VIRGINIA SUPERNATURAL TALES

GHOSTS, WITCHES AND EERIE DOINGS

Also by George Holbert Tucker
  More Tidewater Landfalls
  Tidewater Landfalls
  Norfolk Highlights
  A Goodly Heritage: A History of Jane Austen's Family
  The Jane Austen Companion (contributor)

VIRGINIA SUPERNATURAL TALES

GHOSTS, WITCHES AND EERIE DOINGS

by GEORGE HOLBERT TUCKER
WITH AN INTRODUCTION BY PARKE ROUSE JR.

THE
DONNING COMPANY
PUBLISHERS
NORFOLK/VIRGINIA BEACH

For Elizabeth

Acknowledgements

I wish to acknowledge the following for help in preparing this book: *The Virginian-Pilot* of Norfolk, *The Richmond Times-Dispatch,* and *The Baltimore Sun* for permitting me to use material originally appearing in their papers; U. S. Senator Harry Flood Byrd, Jr., and Virginius Dabney of Richmond for checking out genealogical details concerning stories relating to their ancestors; Parke Rouse, Jr., for writing the introduction, and former Virginia Governor Colgate W. Darden, Jr., for his enthusiastic encouragement.

Cover design by Debbi Pillar

Contents

Introduction

The lure of ghosts is felt by people of all ages. Who hasn't sat around a campfire, as a child, listening to ghost stories? Or frightened visiting cousins with predictions of eerie visitations of "the family ghost" or the spirit of Grandmother So-and-So?

When Virginia was settled, superstition was widespread. Europe had only partly emerged from the long night of the Middle Ages, and the widespread belief in the supernatural led to ghost stories galore. Even more superstitious were the blacks who came as slaves from Africa. In those days, "black magic," voodooism, and "conjuring" were very real to many people. In his fascinating *A Word-Book of Virginia Folk Speech,* published in Richmond in 1907, Dr. Bennett Green listed hundreds of superstitions he had heard from the lips of Tidewater Virginians, both white and black. Many of these persist.

The ghost story flourished in the colonial world, and in the older houses of Virginia it's doing pretty well even in this era of science and skepticism. Nearly every old Virginia house I've known has its resident ghost—or ghostess. The late Mrs. Marguerite duPont Lee collected many in her *Virginia Ghosts,* which remains in demand and in print long years after it was written.

Now George Tucker has written more of these legends in book form. In brisk prose, seasoned with dialogue, he captures many stories you'll hear on winter nights from Accomac to Cumberland Gap. They make good reading, indeed. From his years as the "Tidewater Landfalls" columnist for Norfolk's *The Virginian-Pilot,* he has wide knowledge of Virginia's ghosts, witches, and eerie doings. And with it, he captures something of the flavor of past times—something of the triumphs and tragedies which flow together in the stream we call history. It's a fascinating addition to Virginia's recorded folklore, and good reading, too. George Tucker has done it again.

Parke Rouse, Jr.

The Wraith
At The
Sashless Window

An article headed "House in Jackson Ward Had Weird Visitors in Past," which appeared in the *Richmond Times-Dispatch* on Sunday, January 23, 1921, recounts one of Virginia's strangest ghost stories.

The narrator, Dr. C. A. Bryce, a well-known Richmond physician of his time, had been summoned many years before he recorded the eerie incident to the bedside of a patient in the then-suburban section of Jackson Ward. It was past midnight on a damp and chilly November evening, and as the doctor felt reluctant to hitch up his horse and phaeton at that hour, he accompanied the man who had come for him on foot.

When the two men reached a sparsely built-up street near the sick man's house the doctor noticed that his companion was taking a roundabout way. Thinking this a bit unusual, Dr. Bryce asked the man his reason for avoiding the direct route and was told that the latter did not like to pass after nightfall what he believed was a haunted house in the next block.

Anxious to reach his patient as quickly as possible, Dr. Bryce insisted on their taking the direct route. Just as the two men came abreast of the supposedly haunted house a sudden shifting of the clouds unveiled a full moon that clearly highlighted every detail of the suspected premises.

The house, Dr. Bryce observed, was a large, dilapidated wooden building, its facade partially obscured by two irregularly shaped cedar trees. A closer examination showed that many of the second-story windows were sashless, while the front door stood partially open on the dark hallway beyond, from which came sounds of occasional banging doors.

As there was no time for further investigation, the doctor and his companion continued to the house of the sick man. On his way back home alone, however, Dr. Bryce paused longer in front of the mysterious house to examine it more minutely. Everything was exactly as it had been before. But while Dr. Bryce was standing in the deserted moonlit street he suddenly saw a small white figure flit across the ruined front porch and disappear through the open front door into the dark hall. Even then, Dr. Bryce's suspicions were not aroused sufficiently to investigate further, for he rationalized that what he had seen could either have been an optical illusion or an unidentified night-prowling animal.

Dr. Bryce's opinion was radically revised six months later, however, when he was again called to the bedside of the same patient he had visited on the night he thought he had seen the ghostly figure enter the deserted house. The night of his second visit also happened to coincide with the full moon, and as he passed the grim-looking dwelling, he distinctly saw a pale-faced young woman dressed in a white nightgown standing at one of the sashless upstairs windows. When the doctor looked up at her in astonishment, a high wind that was blowing suddenly disheveled the young woman's long dark hair, covering her face for a moment. Then the figure disappeared.

In order to be sure that he had not seen an actual person, Dr. Bryce persuaded a friend to accompany him to the house the next morning. A careful investigation of the premises only proved that no human beings had been in the place for a long time as the thick dust and cobwebs that covered all of the rooms were undisturbed.

After that, Dr. Bryce made diligent inquiries throughout the neighborhood in an effort to solve the mystery. The closest he could come to an explanation was that the house had been occupied many years ago by three well-to-do foreigners who kept to themselves and made no acquaintances. They had come there suddenly and disappeared as abruptly, neither selling nor leasing the property, but abandoning it.

Meanwhile, five years passed. Then one day Dr. Bryce was called to the bedside of an old Negro who lived a hermit's existence in a little cabin in the rear of the lot adjacent to the abandoned house.

Upon entering the cabin, the doctor immediately recognized the old man as a patient for whom he had prescribed many years before, at which time the old Negro had paid him with a gold French coin, giving no definite reason for having it in his possession. Feeling that the old man might be able to tell him something concerning the mysterious house, Dr. Bryce asked him the direct question. At first the old Negro was reluctant to talk, but he finally told the doctor this story:

"Many years ago," he said, "when the cornfields were all around where these houses and streets are now, three or four big houses were standing in these fields and the one you're talking about was one of them. I was a boy then and the house became vacant and was closed for a year or two. Then one day I noticed that people were living in it.

"My mother lived in this cabin then, and a few days after the people had moved in, a lady came down to see about employing her. My mother found out the family was made up of a gentleman, his wife, and a daughter, and they had three women servants they had brought with them from where they came. They were rich people and hired my mother and me, besides keeping the three women they already had. They were foreigners, for when they talked to each other, we couldn't understand them, but the servants could.

"They didn't go out in the street much, but sometimes they'd send for a carriage and be driven about mostly at night. Their house was well furnished and they wore fine clothes and had plenty of jewelry and everything else they wanted. The young lady, we called her Miss Josephine, was very pretty and she was the only one who ever went out on the streets much. She'd take long walks almost every day by herself.

"One day her father called me into his room and asked me, 'Petaire (my name was Peter, but he always called me Petaire), have you seen any man walking with my daughter at any time?'

"I said, 'No, sir,' and I hadn't.

"But I knew trouble was brewing if he was that suspicious, and sure enough, one day I saw a finely dressed, handsome man meet her in Capitol Square, and they walked along together slowly talking their language I couldn't understand, but anybody could see they were lovers.

" 'Twant long after that before I saw this same man come up to the house and knock on the door. I said to myself he ain't going to get a welcome from the boss, but Miss Josephine met him and begged him to go back before anyone saw him. I never did know how it all happened, but her father came to the door and invited him in, and then there were hard words and he took his leave. The servants told my mother the young man asked for satisfaction as he was leaving, and her father told him he would meet him in New Orleans. They said that meant a duel.

"In a few days her father left to be gone for a week or two, he said, and after he left Miss Josephine took to her bed. Her father didn't come back, but one day when she was reading the paper she turned mighty pale and just fell over in a dead faint. Her mother grabbed up the paper and screamed like somebody wild. They were both sick for a long time.

"I 'spose the young man was killed, maybe both of them, but that's all I ever heard of either of the men. Then one morning the mistis called us all together in Miss Josephine's room, and she was lying in bed and smiling and talking out of her head. We could see she was dying, and just before she went she said, 'Tell Henri I'll always be waiting for him at the window,' and she took one long breath and was gone."

The old Negro then told Dr. Bryce they had shipped the young woman's body away for burial, and that her mother and the servants packed up and left in a few days. After that, the old house stood deserted, the only sounds ever heard from it being the creaking of loose shutters or the slamming of doors as the wind swept through its empty rooms.

"This," Dr. Bryce concluded, "was a most unsatisfactory story that left me in the dark as to the identity of these people, but it did assure me that within the walls of that old building had been scenes of love and sorrow, mystery and death—secrets locked forever in the graves of these actors long gone."

Eighteen Pennies Worth
Of Time

What is perhaps the earliest recorded case of extrasensory perception in Virginia appears in *The Secret Diary of William Byrd of Westover 1709-1712*, edited by Louis B. Wright and Marion Tinling.

The episode, in which a strange, prophetic dream played an important role, began on March 22, 1710, at Shirley, the ancestral home of the Hill and Carter families on the north side of the James River in Charles City County, Virginia.

Byrd and an "abundance of company," including Benjamin Harrison, III, of Berkeley Plantation (1673-1710), a member of the Governor's Council, were present. After a dinner of "bacon and fowl," eight of the gentlemen present, including Byrd and Harrison, played at cricket on the riverside lawn of the mansion, at which time it was noticed that Harrison "looked exceedingly red a great while after it."

Before dawn the next morning, on March 23, 1710, eighteen days before his death, Harrison became ill. His condition did not improve, and the next day an "express" was sent to the Reverend Charles Anderson, the minister of Westover Parish, who was staying with Byrd at Westover, to come as quickly as possible to the sick man's bedside.

The news of Harrison's illness spread rapidly because of his high political eminence in Colonial circles, and in a few days many of his relatives, some of whom were among the most prominent in the colony, were keeping a round-the-clock vigil at his bedside at Berkeley.

Byrd's turn came on March 31, 1710, when he and Nathaniel Burwell, Harrison's brother-in-law, and the Reverend Mr. Anderson sat up all night with him. The next morning at breakfast, Burwell's wife told the assembled company of a strange dream she had experienced during the night.

"It is remarkable," Byrd wrote in his diary, "that Mrs. Burwell dreamed this night that she saw a person that with money scales weighed time and declared that there was no more than 18 pennies worth of time to come, which seems to be a dream of some significance either concerning the world or a sick person."

That was nine days after Harrison had been stricken during the pre-dawn hours of March 23, 1710. From then on his condition became worse.

On Sunday, April 9, 1710, Harrison expressed a desire to eat partridge and Byrd sent him a brace of them. After eating one, Harrison slept uneasily for a while, and when Byrd and his family visited Berkeley that afternoon after dinner, they found a "very melancholy family" gathered around the sick man's bedside.

Finally, at four o'clock the next morning according to a significant entry in Byrd's diary, just as the darkness was beginning to dissolve over the lower reaches of the James River, Harrison awoke and implored his sister, Mrs. Philip Ludwell of Greenspring, who was seated at his bedside, to open the door of his room, adding desperately that "he wanted to go out and could not go until the door was opened and as soon as the door was opened he died."

It was exactly eighteen days after Harrison was stricken in the early morning hours following the cricket match on the lawn of Shirley. Mrs. Burwell's "18 pennies worth of time" had run its prophetic course.

The Scream
From The Fire

Two cryptic lines of blank verse carved on a tombstone in Old Saint Paul's churchyard in Norfolk, Virginia, are the clues to a tragedy that took place there in 1823, a tragedy that sent psychic vibrations across the Atlantic Ocean to the harbor of Genoa, Italy.

The story began a decade before the dreadful event when David Duncan, a serious-minded young seafaring man, began lodging with Mrs. Ann Shirley, a widow who operated a nautical boarding house, when his ship was in Norfolk for any length of time.

Mrs. Shirley was the mother of an only child, a daughter, Martha, who was almost ten years younger than Duncan. Nevertheless, a romance developed, and finally, when he had advanced to the point of becoming the captain of his own vessel, they were engaged to be married.

Duncan married Martha Shirley in Norfolk on October 20, 1820, after which he took her on a wedding journey to Mediterranean ports aboard the *Sea Witch,* the cargo schooner of which he was master.

After returning to Norfolk, the *Sea Witch* was sent to a dockyard for refitting. Duncan and his wife settled down in third-story rooms above a bakery on Wide Water Street for the only short period of domestic happiness they were ever to experience ashore. During that time Mrs. Duncan gave birth to twins, a boy named David for his father, and a girl named Ann for the young bride's mother.

When the *Sea Witch* had been overhauled, Duncan took on a cargo of lumber, barrel staves and hides, and prepared to cross the Atlantic once more. That time he reluctantly left his wife and two children behind. Not long afterward tragedy struck.

On May 12, 1823, a fire broke out in the bakery beneath the rooms where Mrs. Duncan and her two children were living. The structure was built of wood and was quickly destroyed. Mrs. Duncan and her children were trapped when a rickety staircase, their only means of escape, collapsed. They lost their lives in the fire.

The night of the tragedy found the *Sea Witch* anchored in Genoa harbor. Most of the crew had rowed ashore for relaxation in the wine shops along the waterfront, but Duncan had remained aboard. It was a moonless night and only the distant twinkling lights of the city and the beams from the lighthouse at the entrance of the harbor relieved the darkness.

Duncan was sitting quietly in his cabin reading from the eighteenth century poet Edward Young's *Night Thoughts on Life, Death, and Immortality,* a favorite book. When he reached the lines where the poet described Death as an "insatiate archer," he was suddenly aware of a briskly burning fire at the foot of the ship's mainmast. Tossing down the volume he hurried to investigate.

As he approached the fire it grew fiercer, and he was startled when he recognized his young wife, clutching their two babies, in the midst of the flames. Then his horror was intensified when he clearly heard her scream, "David! David! Save us! Save us!" With that, the mysterious fire vanished and all was dark and quiet again.

Duncan was beside himself with fear and apprehension, but in those days of slow communication nothing could be learned concerning his family's welfare until the *Sea Witch* docked in Norfolk. It was then that he heard the details of the tragedy and the additional fact that what had been left of Martha Duncan and her two children had been buried in a single grave in Saint Paul's churchyard.

Duncan placed a flat, raised tombstone with the following inscription over their grave: "Mrs. M. A. E. Duncan Wife of D. Duncan Ob. 12th May 1823 AE 19 Also Her Two Infant Children."

Then, underneath, he had the tombstone maker carve the two prophetic lines of blank verse he had been reading when he saw the frightful fiery vision aboard the *Sea Witch* in Genoa harbor. They read:

Insatiate archer, could not one suffice?
Thy shaft flew thrice and thrice my peace was slain.

Joan Wright— Virginia's First Witch

Joan Wright, a native of Hull, England, had the dubious distinction of being the first person to be legally accused of practicing the Black Arts in Virginia. Joan, who was single when she came to the colony around 1610, married Robert Wright, a sawyer by trade, who had arrived aboard the *Swan* two years earlier.

According to the testimony given by Mrs. Isabel Perry during Joan's trial for witchcraft at Jamestown on September 11, 1626, before Sir George Yeardley and members of his council, Joan was already well acquainted with the works of the Prince of Darkness before she left England for Virginia.

In making her deposition before the General Court, Mistress Perry told the governor and the council members that Goodwife Wright had taken her into her confidence on two occasions concerning witchcraft in which she was a party while still in England.

On the first occasion when Joan, who was then employed as a dairy maid, was churning butter, a woman supposedly in league with the Devil came to the house of her mistress, "whereupon she by directions from her dame Clapt the Chirne staffe to the bottom of the Chirne and clapt her hands across the top of it by wch means the witch was not (able) to stire owt of the place where she was for the space of six howers after wch time good wiefe Wright desired her dame to ask the woman why she did not gett her gone, whereupo(n) the witche fell down on her knees and asked her forgiveness and saide her hande was in the Chirne and could not stire before her maid lifted upp the staffe of the Chirne wch the said good wiefe Wright did, and the witche went awaye, but to her perception ye witche had both her handés at libertie, and this good wiefe Wright affirmeth to be trewe."

On another occasion, Mistress Perry deposed "good wiefe Wright told her, that she was at Hull her dame beinge sick suspected her selfe to be bewitched, and told good wiefe Wright of it, whereupon by directione from her dame, That at the cominge of a woman, wch was suspected, to take a horshwe (horseshoe) and flinge it into the oven and when it was red hott, To flinge it into her dames urine, and so long as the horsewe (horseshoe) was hott, the witch was sick at the harte, And when the Irone was colde she was well againe, And this good wiefe Wright affirmeth to be trwe (true) alsoe."

Before this gossip was passed on to the governor and council, however, Joan Wright had more or less established herself as a mischief maker in the Virginia colony. At first she and her husband had settled at Kecoughtan, now the City of Hampton, Virginia, at the mouth of the James River, where Joan, according to testimony given later at her trial, was "Accompted a witch amongst them all at Kickotan," and where she also acquired an unenviable reputation for supposedly bewitching a neighbor's poultry because he "would sell her none."

By 1626, Joan and her husband and their two children had moved to Surry County on the south side of the James River opposite Jamestown. Still up to her old tricks, Joan had then become such a public nuisance she was hailed before the General Court.

The first witness against her, one Lieutanant Giles Allington, deposed that Joan had become enraged when his pregnant wife refused her services as a midwife because she was left-handed. When Allington brought in a right-handed midwife to deliver the baby, Joan "went awaye from his howse very much discontented," after which Allington, his wife, and the newborn infant fell gravely ill, presumably because Joan had cast a spell on them in retaliation, and although Allington and his wife eventually recovered, the child "fell into extreeme payne the space of five weeks and so departed."

Another witness, Thomas Jones, deposed that "Sargeant Booth told him yt goodwief Wright would have had som what of him, wch the saide Sargeant Booth either would nott or could nott give her, and as this deponent thinketh it was a piece of fflesh, And after the said Sargeant Booth went foorth with his peece, and cam to good game and very fayre to shoote at, But for a large tyme after he could never kill any thinge."

Over the years, Joan had been more or less successful in predicting the deaths of her enemies or neighbors, and on one occasion when a woman confided in her that she had "a cross man to my husband," Joan had replied knowingly "be content for thow shalte shortlie burie him (wch cam to pass)."

Still another witness, Robert Thresher, testified that when he refused to give Joan some young tobacco plants, she used the Black Arts to cause such a heavy downpour in the night that "all his plants were drowned."

Daniel Watkins, another witness, then testified that a few months before the trial took place he was at Mistress Perry's husband's plantation, where Thresher "had a cowple of henns pourposinge to send them over to El(i)zabeth Arundle And good wiefe Wright beinge there in place, saide to Robert Thresher, why do you keepe these henns heere tyed upp, The maide you mean to send them to will be dead before the henns come to her."

The fact that the young woman, who was a servant in the governor's household at Jamestown, had actually died before Thresher could deliver the poultry, added weight to the accusations, and the justices proceeded with the depositions.

At that juncture Mistress Perry, whose testimony concerning Joan's earlier dabbling in witchcraft when she was a servant girl in England has already been quoted, was called on as a witness. Mistress Perry, who obviously was not one of Joan's great admirers, told the court, among other things, that Joan had been enraged at a maidservant for taking a log of lightwood out of the fort, and after threatening the frightened girl "that yf she did nott bringe the light woode againe she would make her daunce starke naked and the next morninge ye lightwood was founde in the forte."

Mistress Perry then added that a friend, Dorothy Behethlan, had asked her why she allowed Joan to come to her house, "sayinge she was a very bad woman," after which Mistress Perry "Chid the saide Good wiefe Wright, And said unto her, yf thow knowest thyselfe Cleare of what she Charges thee, why dost thow not complaine And cleare

21

thyselfe of the same, To whom good wiefe Wright replied, god forgive them, and so made light of it."

With these damaging depositions on record, Joan's husband was then asked if he could corroborate any of the testimony, but he only said he had been married to Joan for sixteen years and knew "no thing of her touchinge the Crimes she was accused of."

At that point the record of Virginia's first witchcraft hearing ends abruptly, there being no existing record of the court in connection with the evidence that shows that the case was ever resolved. Later, however, the General Court levied a fine of one hundred pounds of tobacco on Joan for an unspecified cause, and although no mention of witchcraft exists in the entry, it is assumed that it was imposed as a warning to Joan to curtail her dabblings in the Black Arts.

Mike Hardy's
Last Confession

One of Virginia's most unusual ghost stories was taken down several years ago from the recollections of a doctor concerning the deathbed confession of a patient he attended during the early years of his medical practice. The doctor, whose name is not essential to the story, was a general practitioner in the city of Portsmouth for almost half a century until his death in the 1940s.

Early one spring morning in 1905 he received an urgent two-fold message. The bearer told him that a patient of his, a sixty-year-old bachelor named Mike Hardy who was ill with tuberculosis, had taken a turn for the worse. He then urged the doctor not only to call on his patient immediately, but to bring along a priest because the sick man, a Catholic, wished to receive the Rite of Extreme Unction.

Mike Hardy was a more or less legendary figure in the Gosport section of Portsmouth, where he lived and where he was looked upon by the poor and needy as a saint for his good deeds. But he had not always been that kind of man. It was well known that before a miraculous change had taken place in his life a few years after his return from the Civil War, he had been the most notorious rakehell in the community in which he was born and where he had grown into early manhood.

The doctor responded immediately to the urgent summons, stopping on the way at the rectory of St. Paul's Catholic Church near his home to pick up a priest. Then the two of them drove to Hardy's house in the doctor's buggy.

When they arrived and were admitted by Hardy's housekeeper, they discovered the sick man had lapsed into a coma. But that did not stop the priest from performing his duty, and, with the aid of the doctor, who was also a Catholic, he anointed the sick man for death.

Shortly after the rite was administered, however, Hardy regained consciousness, and after a while he was able to talk weakly, but distinctly. Although he had apparently been insensible at the time he had received the last rites of the church, he seemed to know that they had been administered, and he thanked the priest for having performed them. Then realizing that the doctor was standing on the other side of his bed, he reached up and took his hand and thanked him for being so faithful in his attendance. After that, Hardy smiled and closed his eyes and was silent for some time. Then he began to speak.

"My dear friends," he said in a weak but firm voice, "I am happy you are here for I want to tell both of you something that I have never revealed to another person." Then, looking at the priest, Hardy added, "I didn't even confess it many years ago when I came back into the church, but that's all right, for I know God has forgiven me."

There was a long pause, then Hardy continued, "Both of you know, by hearsay at least, what kind of a man I was during my younger days. You also know, I suppose, that I served for four years in the Confederate Army before returning to Portsmouth again. But that isn't really what I want to tell you."

Hardy was quiet for a few moments, then spoke again. "Women and liquor were all that I lived for before the war and during the time I served in the army, and I had no scruples about how I got either of them, just so long as they were plentiful. You might also have heard that I was a crack shot in my youth, and that stood me in good stead, for they made a sharpshooter of me and I was a good one and killed many a man during those four years.

"Then, two or three days before General Lee surrendered at Appomattox, I was sitting high up in the branches of a big oak tree. I was drunk and was feeling bitter about everything. My parents and the only girl I ever really cared for had all died while I was away, and I was also mighty unhappy about how the war was turning out with me on the losing side.

"A terrible hatred boiled up in me and I felt if I could kill just one more Yankee, I could go home satisfied. Well, almost as if by magic, my wish was immediately gratified. I looked down the road and saw a young fellow with curly red hair, wearing a new blue uniform, come out of the woods and stand there basking in the bright sunlight. He was so full of himself he even did a little jig there in the road, never thinking that I was watching him.

"As I said before, I felt I just had to kill one more Yankee before quitting, and when I saw that young fellow I knew he was the one. And while he was capering there in the road, I raised my gun, put a bead on him, and pulled the trigger. I'll never forget the look of amazement that came over that young fellow's face when the bullet hit him. His eyes popped wide open and he looked like he couldn't believe what had happened. Then he dropped down dead."

Mike Hardy lapsed into silence for some time, then he began again. "Well, I walked back to Portsmouth, where I kept up my evil ways. But somehow I just couldn't get that young fellow and what I'd done to him off my mind. And it came near driving me crazy.

"Then one day I was passing St. Paul's, where I had served at mass when I was a little shaver and which I had avoided for years, and I had a tremendous urge to go in and ask God's forgiveness for what I had done. There were only a few vigil lights burning near the altar, and the place was dim and quiet. So I knelt down in a pew, closed my eyes, and tried to pray. But the words just stuck in my throat.

"I was about to give up in despair, when I happened to look toward the confessional and saw a faint light behind the curtain where the priest sits. When I saw that I naturally supposed he was there, so I got up and went into the confessional and poured out my sorrow, trying to make my confession as complete as possible.

"When I was through, I waited a few moments for advice and possible absolution. But nothing was said, and I was beginning to feel uneasy when a strange, unearthly voice came to me from where I had supposed the priest was sitting.

" 'I have long since forgiven you for that terrible thing you did to me on that beautiful spring day,' the voice said. 'I was young and full of life and was looking forward to going home to be with my parents and family again when you deliberately killed me. But you really did me a favor, you know, for if you hadn't done that to me, I wouldn't be here now to warn you that if you don't change your evil ways, you'll never be able to go where I am now.' "

Mike Hardy paused again, and the tears welled up in his eyes. "At first I didn't know what to think, so I went back to the pew and sat down again. And when I looked toward the confessional I saw the light that had been there was gone. Then sensing that someone was near me, I looked in the other direction and saw him—that red-haired, blue-clad boy standing there. When he saw that I was aware of his presence, he smiled. Then he vanished."

By then, Mike Hardy's voice was growing faint, but he made one last effort. "My friends," he said, almost in a whisper, "I am not afraid to die, for since that experience I have tried to live a decent life and think of others rather than myself. And I also want you to know that although you can't see him, that boy I killed is here in this room, waiting to take me with him when I go."

That was all. The doctor and the priest stared at one another in silent amazement, and when they looked back at Mike Hardy again, he had turned his head on the pillow and had died with a radiant smile on his face.

The General's Last Appearance

Cleve, the ancestral home of the Carter family in King George County, Virginia, was the setting for a strange supernatural happening that took place a little after eight o'clock on the evening of June 8, 1816.

The handsome old rose brick house was built around the middle of the eighteenth century by Charles Carter of Cleve, a son of Robert Carter of Corotoman in Lancaster County, known in Virginia history as King Carter because of his wealth and imperious nature. Remaining in the Carter family until just before the Civil War, the stately old Georgian country house, one of Virginia's great plantation homes, was burned on January 17, 1917.

At the time the eerie happening took place it was the home of Colonel St. Leger Landon Carter, a longtime member of the Virginia Senate who devoted his leisure hours to literary pursuits. One of the Colonel's sisters, Lucy Landon Carter, was the wife of General John Minor, III, the principal in the ghost story.

Born in 1761 at Topping Castle, his ancestral home in Caroline County, Virginia, Minor joined the Continental forces when he was fifteen, served throughout the Revolution, and was present at the surrender of Cornwallis at Yorktown. After the war, Minor studied law under Chancellor George Wythe, then settled in Fredericksburg, Virginia, where he achieved an enviable reputation for legal knowledge and eloquence. His military title dated from the

War of 1812, during which he was a general in the Virginia line.

Minor was an intimate friend of James Monroe, and when the latter was a candidate for the Presidency in 1816, Minor served as a member of the Electoral College that cast the vote of the state of Virginia for Monroe. As usual, the Virginia Electoral College delegates met in Richmond, and while it was sitting the citizens gave a testimonial dinner in its honor on the evening of June 8, 1816, at the Swan Tavern, a famous Richmond hostelry located near the State Capitol.

Minor was to have been one of the principal speakers, but when his time came he was stricken with apoplexy and was carried into another room where he died a few minutes after eight o'clock.

Meanwhile Minor's wife and other members of her family were sitting in the parlor at Cleve. One of the guests was her brother-in-law, William McFarland, a lawyer and amateur poet. A few minutes after eight o'clock, McFarland excused himself and left the parlor to go up to his room, but when he entered the hall he received a shock. At that moment General Minor, wearing his riding clothes and a shiny beaver hat, entered the front door and walked up the broad staircase to the second floor without acknowledging him.

Alarmed because the General seemed unduly preoccupied, McFarland returned to the parlor and told the company what he had seen, only to be laughed at and assured it was an impossibility as the General was known to be in Richmond at a banquet and was not expected to return to Cleve for several days.

McFarland was insistent, however, and Mrs. Minor was finally persuaded to send a servant on horseback to Richmond the next morning to learn if anything out of the ordinary had happened to her husband.

He was not long in discovering the truth, for about halfway between Cleve and Richmond he met a mounted group of the General's friends who were accompanying his body back to Fredericksburg. He also learned that a little after eight o'clock on the previous evening when McFarland had seen the general's ghost in the hall of Cleve, Minor had died in the Swan Tavern in Richmond.

The Devil's Spawn

During the early years of the eighteenth century a handsome but dissolute young farmer who lived in Prince George County was one of the many suitors of a pretty young girl who lived on a nearby farm. His bad habits and evil temper were decidedly against him, and the girl gave his attentions short shrift until a mysterious right-about-face in her attitude caused her family and friends to believe someone had cast a spell on her. They were right, for the Devil, always anxious to add another unit of population to his infernal kingdom, happened to pass that way just about that time, and after sizing up the young farmer's predicament, decided to do something about it.

One dark, stormy night the young farmer was sitting in a drunken state before the fire in a crossroads tavern, his only companion an almost empty bottle of brandy. He had again been rebuffed by the pretty young girl, with whom he was madly infatuated, and had been drinking heavily to drown his troubles.

Suddenly the door opened and a tall, dark, handsome man with flashing eyes strode in. Removing his greatcoat and rakishly cocked hat, he tossed them on a chair, then rapped loudly with the butt of his whip on a table to attract the attention of the innkeeper. After his bumper of rum was served, the stranger pulled a chair to the fire and sat beside the moody young man. Then he spoke.

"Pardon me, my friend, but you seem to be down in the

dumps," he said insinuatingly. "Whatever can be the reason?"

That was all the besotted young man needed. He began to pour our his frustrations concerning his unsuccessful courtship to the dark, handsome stranger. When he had finished, his companion tossed off the remaining rum in his glass, wiped his mouth with the back of his hand, and spoke in an offhand manner.

"I'm a stranger in these parts and won't be tarrying long, but maybe I can help you while I'm here." Then, after a pause, he added, "I'm rather knowledgeable in matters of the heart, and maybe I can give you a few hints that will make that pretty girl show you more favor."

Ready to grasp at any straw of encouragement, the sottish young man asked anxiously for more details.

"Well," the stranger with the flashing eyes continued, "it all depends on how much you actually want the young woman."

"My God!" the young man blurted out, "I'd give my soul to the Devil to get that girl!"

"Mmm! That changes the picture most satisfactorily," the stranger said, "but before I can guarantee to be of any help, we'd better draw up a contract of some sort."

"Willingly!" the young man cried, taking a swig from the brandy bottle.

"In that case, it will be easy," the stranger said with a persuasive chuckle. "I'll put the terms in writing, then we'll sign it. After that, I'll give you a magic powder...."

"And what will that do?" the besotted young farmer interrupted.

"Oh, just put it into something she'll drink, and that will make her see things in an entirely different light," the stranger said archly.

"Agreed!" the young man called out. The stranger ordered the innkeeper to bring paper, ink, and a turkey feather quill. These were brought, and when he and the farmer were alone again, the stranger hastily scribbled a short paragraph in which he agreed to furnish a love potion to the infatuated young man in exchange for his soul.

"That last phrase is only a matter of form," the stranger remarked dryly, "but since they were your own words we'll use them to save the trouble of thinking up any others."

Disregarding the stranger's remarks, the young man grabbed the quill, dipped it into the inkpot, and scribbled his name below the paragraph. Then the man with the flashing eyes took the quill and inscribed the word "Beelzebub" with a flourish beneath the young farmer's signature.

At that moment, in a sudden sobering flash, the young man realized what he had done and he began to remonstrate loudly. But the mysterious stranger merely handed him a small packet. Then, taking up the contract, he put on his greatcoat and hat and strode out into the night.

The young man sat in stupefied silence for some time, then gradually fell into a drunken slumber. When he awoke several hours later he settled his reckoning, picked up the packet, and headed for the stable for his horse.

Time passed, and although the young farmer continued to worry about the contract he had rashly signed with the stranger, he finally began to assure himself that maybe he had not read the agreement too carefully. And it was not long before he had rationalized the situation to the point where he decided to give the love potion a try. Riding over to the girl's house, he said he had come to tell her of his decision to abandon his courtship. When she seemed pleased, he asked that they have a glass of wine together to part as friends. Never suspecting trickery, the girl told him he would find wine and glasses in the next room. When he went to fetch them, he slyly stirred the potion into the glass of wine intended for the girl whose hand he hoped to win. Then they drank together and he rode away.

Almost immediately, to the surprise of everyone, the girl began to hanker for the young farmer, and it was not long before she agreed to marry him. After the wedding they went to live on his farm, and for a time an uncertain peace prevailed. Naturally the young woman wanted children, but her husband was so jealous of anyone who might divert her attention from himself that he swore there would never be any babies if he had anything to do with the matter. Despite these protests, however, the young woman became pregnant. When her husband learned of her condition, he beat her unmercifully, calling out, "I'd rather have a devil in this house than that brat you're bearing!"

When his wife begged for mercy, he grabbed up the baby clothes she was making and threw them into the fire. At that moment the flames became devil's claws as they tore at the bricks in the back of the fireplace, while a fiendish laugh echoed down the chimney.

From then on the young farmer began to drink excessively and spent more and more time gambling at the tavern in the company of rowdy companions. Finally, when her time came, the young wife enlisted the help of a midwife. When the baby was born it turned out to be a red-eyed little monster covered with hard black scales, with claws on its hands and feet instead of nails, two small, horn-like protuberances jutting from its forehead, and a stub of a tail.

Horrified, the young mother begged the midwife not to say anything about the unusual brat, but the woman was a gossip and the news soon spread throughout the neighborhood. People began calling at the farmhouse hoping to catch a glimpse of the monster, but the mother foiled their curiosity by keeping him locked in a closet.

Meanwhile, the husband got wind of what had happened. He disappeared, and it was presumed he was dead. But he had only run off to another part of Virginia. Eventually his curiosity got the best of him, however, and he returned home to verify the rumors.

The night he staggered back home was dark and stormy. He burst in upon his frightened wife, who sat weeping before the fireplace, and demanded to see the child. When she refused to produce it, he grabbed up a poker and began beating her severely. A sudden ear-splitting yell came from the closet where the monster was secreted. Throwing down the poker, the man tried to open the closet. It was locked. He seized an axe and broke down the door.

At that moment the monster leaped into the center of the room, pointed a claw-tipped finger at the horrified man, and called out, "All right! You said you'd rather have a devil in the house than a regular baby, so here I am!" After an ominous pause during which lightning flashed through the windows and thunder rumbled over the rooftop, he yelled even louder, "What's more, you've done enough harm on earth, and my Daddy will soon be here to drag you down to Hell!"

There was a sudden flash, and the monster disappeared in a cloud of sulphurous smoke. When it had cleared, there stood the mysterious stranger in greatcoat and rakishly cocked hat, holding aloft in the long, pointed fingers of his right hand the contract signed by the farmer and himself. There was a long pause. Then he spoke.

"You have come to the end of your rope, my friend," he said in a menacing voice, adding with a chuckle, "and I have come to collect my bargain."

At that point the farmer fell down dead. A moment later a tiny bat-like creature flew up from his open mouth and began beating its wings against one of the windows in an effort to escape. Letting out a laugh, the mysterious stranger walked casually in that direction, grabbed the wildly fluttering creature, wrapped the contract around it, and then disappeared up the chimney.

That was too much for the poor abused wife, who ran out of the house into the storm. But she didn't run far, for a sudden blaze of light behind her caused her to look over her shoulder. In a flash, she realized the house was on fire. And when the wildly dancing flames were through, there was nothing left of it but an upright chimney and smoldering coals in the cellar.

The Ghost
Who Was Comforted

Major Joel West Flood, the maternal grandfather of
Harry Flood Byrd, Sr., Virginia's governor from 1926 to
1930 and United States Senator from Virginia from 1933 to
1964, was one of the principals, when he was a baby, in what
is perhaps Virginia's tenderest ghost story.

The Floods, an old Virginia family, were descended
from Lieutenant Colonel John Flood, a seventeenth century
member of the Virginia House of Burgesses and the official
Indian interpreter of the colony.

Sometime during the eighteenth century a branch of the
Flood family moved to a plantation called Elton in
Appomattox County, Virginia, a property that was
eventually inherited by Dr. Joel Walker Flood, the
grandfather of Major Joel West Flood.

Major Flood, who was born on January 9, 1839, was the
only child of Colonel Harry DeLaWarr Flood and Mrs. Mary
Elizabeth Trent Flood. His daughter, Miss Eleanor Bolling
Flood, married Richard Evelyn Byrd. They were Senator
Byrd's parents.

Seventeen days after Major Flood's birth, his mother
died at the age of eighteen. Out of kindness to their grief-
stricken son, Colonel Flood's parents took the baby to rear.
His grandmother installed the infant in her large old-
fashioned bedroom and hired an experienced nurse to care
for him.

Dr. Flood, the most prominent physician in the

Appomattox County community, had an extensive practice and was frequently called out at night to attend his patients. On these occasions his wife always left a lamp burning in the downstairs hall and went to bed at her regular time.

One night when Dr. Flood was away, Mrs. Flood awoke from a sound sleep and saw a strange sight through the parting of the heavy silk brocade curtains at the foot of her tester bed. By the light of the smouldering fire on the bedroom hearth she plainly saw the ghost of the baby's mother bending over the crib in which the child was peacefully sleeping. The spirit was obviously in great distress and was weeping bitterly.

Naturally, Mrs. Flood was startled by the apparition and lost no time in getting out of bed. Throwing a dressing gown over her nightdress, she hurriedly left the bedroom, descended the stairs, and waited in the downstairs hall for her husband to return from his late night call. When he arrived, she told him what she had seen, but he politely declined to believe the story, saying she had no doubt dreamed the whole episode. Mrs. Flood was unconvinced, however, and when she continued to see the ghost of the distressed mother bending over the child's crib, she decided to take matters into her own hands.

A few nights afterward, when the doctor was again absent on another late call, Mrs. Flood undressed as usual, went to bed, and waited. A few moments later the weeping ghost of her dead daughter-in-law appeared, bent over the baby's crib, and began to wring her hands in great distress. Summoning up her courage, Mrs. Flood sat up in bed and addressed her ghostly visitor.

"Dear daughter," she said firmly, but tenderly, "I have seen you come and bend over your baby for many nights now, and it is obvious that you are fearful concerning his future."

Then, when the spirit of the young mother turned her tearful face toward Mrs. Flood, the latter continued, "I want to assure you, dear daughter, that everything will be done by my husband and myself to rear your child properly. And it will also be our fervent hope that he will not only grow up to be a credit to us, but will also become as fine and gentle a person as you were when you were among the living."

When Mrs. Flood had finished speaking the ghost of the young mother smiled at her through her tears. Then, after bending tenderly over the sleeping baby one more time, she disappeared and was never seen again.

Fate Knocked
Four Times

Fate knocked four times in quick succession in the life of Hetty Cary before her brief married happiness was shattered by a Federal sharpshooter's bullet.

Hetty was a daughter of Virginia-born Wilson Miles Cary of Baltimore, Maryland. Described by a contemporary as being "fearless as she was beautiful," Hetty was ordered out of Baltimore by the Union forces at the outbreak of the Civil War because she flaunted a Confederate flag from a window of her home at the Federal troops as they marched into the city. Also included in the banishment was Hetty's sister, Jennie, who had incurred the displeasure of the Union authorities by setting James Ryder Randall's stirring poem "Maryland, My Maryland" to an old German melody.

Hetty and Jennie Cary came to Richmond, Virginia, where with their cousin, Constance Cary, later Mrs. Burton Harrison, the author, they organized the "Cary Invincibiles." Their behind-the-line morale-building activities for the Southern cause are a part of the wartime history of the Confederate Capital.

Meanwhile, Hetty had met and fallen in love with Brigadier General John Pegram, an 1854 West Point graduate who had seen service in the West before the outbreak of the Civil War. It was not until late in the war, however, after Hetty's mother had arrived in Richmond from Baltimore, that their wedding took place on January

19, 1865. At that point fate took over, according to well-documented evidence.

Two days before she was married, Hetty visited her cousin Constance Cary to try on her wedding veil. As she turned from the mirror, it crashed to the floor and broke into small fragments, a long-believed omen of misfortune. On the day the couple were married in St. Paul's Episcopal Church near the Virginia State Capitol, then the Capitol of the Confederacy, they were late for the ceremony. Finally, when they arrived in a battered old hack, it was learned that when President Jefferson Davis' carriage had arrived to take them to the church the horses had reared violently and had refused to go forward.

Then, as the bride entered the church, she dropped her lace handkerchief. When she stooped to retrieve it, the tulle veil over her face was badly torn.

After the ceremony, Hetty returned to Petersburg with her husband, where she was honored with a review of General Pegram's division, during which General Robert E. Lee rode at her side.

Again fate reared a warning finger, for Hetty's horse almost knocked down a gaping soldier. When she reigned in the spirited animal and tried to apologize, however, the soldier pulled off his battered old hat and called out gallantly, "Never mind, Miss! You might have rid over me, indeed you might!"

Four days later, on February 6, 1865, before daylight, General Pegram was ordered into action at Hatcher's Run. Around sunset, when he was leading a charge, he was killed instantly by a Minié ball through the heart.

Fearing to break the bad news, Pegram's friends induced Hetty to go to bed, saying it would be late before he could return. The next morning an old gentleman, a civilian, told her the truth and led her into the room under her bedroom where Pegram's body had been placed.

"Kneeling beside the body," her cousin Constance recalled, "she put her hand into the breast of his coat, drawing out first his watch, still ticking, that she had wound for him just before they parted, next a miniature of herself, both stained with blood."

Accompanied by her mother and brother, Hetty returned to Richmond in a freight car with her husband's body. Exactly three weeks after their wedding, his coffin "crossed with a victor's palms," occupied the spot in the chancel of St. Paul's where he had stood to be married. Beside it knelt Hetty swathed in crepe.

General Pegram was buried with military honors in Hollywood Cemetery in Richmond. In concluding her account of the tragedy in her *Recollections Grave and Gay,* Hetty's cousin Constance wrote:

"Snow lay white on the hillsides, the bare trees stretched out their arms above us, the river kept up its ceaseless rush and tumble, so much a part of our daily life in our four years of ordeal that we had grown accustomed to interpret its voice according to our joy or grief."

Catharine Gamble's Warning

If Colonel Robert Gamble, for whom the Gamble's Hill area of modern Richmond, Virginia, takes its name, had heeded his wife's prophetic dream, he might have lived out his Biblical allotment of three score and ten years. When he disregarded her warning, however, he met his fate at the age of fifty-six, when he was one of the Virginia Capital's leading and most useful citizens.

Born in Augusta County, Virginia, in 1754, Gamble was already a successful merchant when war broke out between the American colonies and the Mother Country. Gamble served as an officer throughout the war and took part in many of its battles, including Princeton and Monmouth. He led the assaulting parties at Stony Point and was permanently deafened by the discharge of one of the enemy's cannons that was fired just as he reached it. Later Gamble was taken prisoner in South Carolina and was confined to a British vessel in Charleston harbor.

After the war Gamble married Catharine Grattan (1753-1831), who had migrated from Ireland to Virginia with her parents before the Revolution and settled in Rockbridge County. Catharine Grattan Gamble was described by a contemporary as a woman "of great energy and character," equal to any emergency of frontier life. Once while living in the Virginia back country she rode thirty miles in one night, with her sister's infant on her lap, to warn the outlying settlements of an approach of hostile

Indians.

Robert and Catharine Gamble first set up housekeeping in Staunton, Virginia, where Gamble became a prosperous businessman and lieutenant of the local militia. Early in the 1790s he and his wife moved to Richmond, where Gamble bought a handsome new Federal mansion on the outskirts of the city designed by the celebrated architect Benjamin Latrobe. There he and his family lived for the next decade "in the enjoyment of elegant hospitality." Gamble maintained a generous household, half a dozen servants, a carriage, a "coachee" and a chair, along with a well-equipped stable of thoroughbred carriage and riding horses. One of the latter was responsible for his death.

Gamble was in the habit of riding into Richmond to his countinghouse daily and returning the same way when his business was completed. On the morning of April 12, 1810, when he came down to breakfast, he observed that his wife, who, according to family tradition, was gifted with what is known as second sight, looked depressed. Asked what was distressing her, Catharine Gamble replied, "My dear, you will do me a great favor if you do not venture into the city today." When Gamble asked why, she continued, "I dreamed last night that if you leave this house today you will never enter it alive again."

Discounting his wife's fears, the colonel called for his favorite mount and cantered into Richmond, stopping on the way to his countinghouse to buy a newspaper. A few minutes later as he rode through the warehouse area of Richmond, reading the newspaper, a great bundle of buffalo hides was thrown out of an upper window and landed with a loud thud directly in front of Gamble's spirited horse. Rearing suddenly, the horse threw Gamble to the ground. His head struck a large rock, producing concussion of the brain from which he died in a short time.

Gamble's social position and the suddenness of his death caused great consternation among his friends, and after a consultation it was decided that a party of them would accompany his body home in order to break the sad news to his widow. They were not prepared, however, for what they found. They discovered Catharine Gamble seated solemnly in the middle of the downstairs hall, surrounded by the terrified house servants.

"You see," she said ominously, indicating the colonel's lifeless body as it was being borne in by his friends, "I begged him not to venture into the city today, for I knew if he did he would never return to this house alive."

Then, turning to Gamble's astonished friends, she told them of her dream of the night before. "That is why," she concluded, "when he insisted on going I went upstairs immediately and put on my best black silk dress in order that I would be suitably attired to receive his corpse when it was brought home."

Dancing With
The Devil

Colonel Philip Lightfoot (1689-1748), of Yorktown and Teddington at Sandy Point on the north side of the James River, was the only Virginian, according to tradition, who ever succeeded in outsmarting the Devil.

Proud as Lucifer himself, Lightfoot, one of the wealthiest and most influential Virginians of his day, was descended from an ancient family in Northamptonshire, England, whose surname was supposedly derived from agility in running. In any event, if an old James River story is to be believed, Lightfoot's nimbleness stood him in good stead when he had his memorable terpsichorean contest with the Prince of Darkness.

History gives ample evidence of the colonel's arrogance, the most outstanding instance being the occasion on which he insulted the Speaker of the House of Burgesses. In 1720, Lightfoot was called before the irate members of that body for "Insulting their Speaker at the door...in a haughty manner...uttering indecent and reproachful language to him without any previous discourse with him."

This toploftiness on Colonel Lightfoot's part netted him a stiff fine and the additional humiliation of having to publicly beg the Speaker's pardon. Apparently eating humble pie didn't cause the colonel too much grief, however, for according to the old James River legend he had more than enough haughtiness left in his makeup to outsmart the Old Boy when the mythical dancing contest took place.

To come to the point, there was an extensive marsh on Lightfoot's plantation at Sandy Point that was a favorite nocturnal haunt of the will-o-the-wisps and other minor earthbound subjects of His Satanic Majesty. This did not please the colonel, for he wanted it converted into arable land, but he was at a loss how to proceed on such an extensive project.

Then one evening, according to tradition, when Old Scratch was paying Lightfoot a social call, an amenity he reputedly observed frequently until the famous dancing contest finally put an end to their amicable relationship, the colonel, after informing the Devil of his desire to convert the marsh into good land, elicited His Satanic Majesty's help in performing the operation.

"I'll tell you what I'll do," the Devil said after a brief reflection. "I'll meet you here tomorrow night and we'll decide the issue by a trial of dancing."

When Lightfoot asked for elucidation, the Devil grinned from ear to ear, then continued, "That is easily explained, my friend. If you outdance me, I'll gladly transform the marsh into high and dry ground for you, but if I outdance you, I'll leave the marsh as it is and take you down to Hell with me so I won't have to travel so far when I wish to visit you again."

Smiling in agreement, Lightfoot invited the Devil to have a nightcap with him, after which they shook hands and parted company.

The next night at midnight Lightfoot and the Devil met at the appointed rendezvous, known to this day as Dancing Point, where, by the light of shooting stars and the scraping of diabolical fiddles played by the imps of darkness, they danced round and round. No witnesses were there to cheer them on, but the desire to improve his plantation was sufficient incentive to Lightfoot to make him shake a nimble leg. And despite the supernatural odds against him, when the sun finally peeped over the eastern reaches of the James River the Devil, letting out a wild scream of chagrin, retreated from the contest in disgust, while the colonel, who was still going strong, discovered, much to his pleasure, that the spot formerly occupied by the marsh was a high and dry field.

Nevertheless the Devil had the last laugh after all. For although Lightfoot got his fine tobacco land in place of the marsh, an unsightly barren spot of a hundred yards in circumference where the dancing contest took place, on which nothing could ever be induced to grow again, remained on the colonel's lawn to remind him that it didn't pay to outsmart the Old Boy.

Specter Warns Rector

An unpretentious granite marker in tree-shaded Trinity Episcopal Churchyard in downtown Portsmouth, Virginia, memorializes the last resting place of the Reverend John Braidfoot, the second rector of Portsmouth Parish, who was warned several times by an apparition in white that he would die on a certain day.

Born in the lowlands of Scotland during the middle years of the eighteenth century, Braidfoot received a good classical education before he decided to enter holy orders. He was ordained as a priest of the Established Church early in 1772, and in April of the same year he received a King's Bounty grant providing him with the necessary funds to cross the Atlantic to take up his duties as an Anglican clergyman in the Virginia colony.

Braidfoot was a friend and the successor of the Reverend Charles Smith, the first rector of Portsmouth Parish, who died in 1773, at which time he directed in his will that his manuscripts were to be burned and that he was "to be buried Decently in a plain pine Cophin near a cherry tree bearing about S. W. from the house and upon this Glebe."

Shortly after succeeding the Reverend Charles Smith as rector of Portsmouth Parish, Braidfoot married Blandinah Moseley on March 12, 1773. When the Revolutionary War broke out, Braidfoot, despite his British background, sided with the American colonists and served as a chaplain in the

Second Virginia Regiment from 1778 to 1781.

After the surrender of Lord Cornwallis at Yorktown, Braidfoot resumed his duties as the rector of Portsmouth Parish and continued to reside with his wife and family on the church glebe on the outskirts of Portsmouth. Braidfoot was well liked by his parishioners and spent a great deal of his time in the saddle visiting the sick and afflicted in the remote areas of his jurisdiction.

It was on one of these horseback journeys that Braidfoot first encountered the apparition in white. Braidfoot was riding back to the glebe one dark and stormy evening in 1784 when his horse shied suddenly and appeared dreadfully frightened. Tightening the reins to control the quivering animal, Braidfoot looked down from the saddle and saw the ghostly figure of a white-clad woman standing a few feet away. Stopping his horse, Braidfoot waited for the phantom to speak. A few moments later it raised its right arm, pointed in Braidfoot's direction, and told him that he would die on February 6, 1785. Then it vanished into the windy darkness.

When Braidfoot arrived home, he informed his wife immediately of the experience and the frightful warning. Observing that her husband was visibly shaken, Mrs. Braidfoot tried to comfort him by suggesting that he had dozed off for a few moments while he was riding homeward and had dreamed the unpleasant episode. Braidfoot had not dreamed it, however, for the apparition appeared to him several times during the next few months, each time repeating the dire prophecy.

On February 6, 1785, the date the white-clad specter foretold the rector would die, Mrs. Braidfoot, in order to relieve her husband of the accute tension from which he was obviously suffering, invited a large party of friends to come to the glebe for dinner. As no one present, with the exception of Braidfoot and his wife, knew anything concerning the ghostly apparition and its ominous warnings, a merry time was enjoyed by the guests. During the dinner, however Braidfoot turned suddenly pale, begged to be excused from the table, and went upstairs to his bedroom. When he did not return, his apprehensive wife followed him and discovered his lifeless body sprawled across the bed.

There were no marks of violence on his person, and it was established by everyone present at the subsequent coroner's inquest that he had not committed suicide.

Braidfoot was first buried in an unmarked grave near the cherry tree on the glebe beside his friend and predecessor, the Reverend Charles Smith. Many years later his remains, and those of the Reverend Mr. Smith, were removed to the graveyard of Trinity Episcopal Church in downtown Portsmouth.

The Demented Lover
Of Lake Drummond

One of Virginia's oldest ghost stories is laid in the Great
Dismal Swamp, a primeval marshy area of about six
hundred square miles extending about forty miles southward from Suffolk, Virginia, to Elizabeth City, North
Carolina.

The swamp, known since the earliest Colonial times,
has always borne a sinister reputation. In its center is Lake
Drummond, the background for the ghost story, a large
cypress-bordered body of clear brown water that was
discovered and named in 1677 by William Drummond, the
first Colonial governor of North Carolina. Colonel William
Byrd, II, of Westover, who was one of the Virginia commis-
sioners in 1728 to survey the boundary line between Virginia and North Carolina, is credited with first describing
the area as "dismal," while George Washington, who owned
part of the vast natural wilderness that he described as a
"glorious paradise," sent slaves there in 1763 to build canals
in an effort to drain it.

It took the celebrated Irish poet, Thomas Moore (1779-
1852), one of the literary darlings of fashionable London
society of his time, however, to put the snake-infested,
Spanish-moss-draped area on the literary map. Moore, who
had stopped over in Norfolk, Virginia, in 1803-04 after
accepting the post of admiralty registrar in Bermuda,
accompanied a party of gentlemen on an expedition into the
vast silences of the swamp during his Norfolk visit. It was at

that time that he heard the even-then old legend of the demented lover of Lake Drummond which he later utilized as the basis of a poem frequently found in Victorian anthologies.

No one knows exactly who the original lovers in the legend were, but they must have existed, otherwise there would have been no basis for the story. In any event, according to the most commonly told version of the tale, a beautiful young girl lived sometime during the early part of the eighteenth century with her family on a farm near the Great Dismal Swamp in the area of what was then known as Norfolk County, but is now the City of Chesapeake.

A young man in the neighborhood fell in love with her and asked her to marry him. Immediately after her acceptance, however, tragedy took over. The young girl contracted malaria and died while her lover was temporarily away from the area. When he returned and learned that her funeral had already taken place, he lost his reason and lay in a coma for a long time. Finally, when he regained consciousness, he refused to believe that his sweetheart was dead.

"No," he raved, "she has only wandered off into the swamp in her delirium, and I will go and find her."

Before leaving her parents' home, he told them that if he found her he intended to hide her in a cypress tree hollow to protect her permanently from Death.

Weeks passed as the frantic man plunged deeper and deeper into the vast reaches of the swamp, living on berries and cypress water and sleeping on grassy tussocks in the snake-infested wilderness. Then, late one night, just as he was about to fall off to sleep in a clearing on the edge of Lake Drummond, he saw what was obviously a will-o-the-wisp flitting across the inky surface of the water. Believing it to be his lost sweetheart, he called out frantically for her to come to him, but the flickering light only moved off swiftly in another direction.

During the next few days the deranged man constructed a raft of the dead tree branches that littered the shore of the lake, and when it was completed he waited impatiently for the light to appear again. When this happened, he rowed out toward it. But just as he was about to overtake the baleful glow, the fragile raft disintegrated and the demented lover was drowned.

According to tradition, the lovers were finally united in death. For since that time countless numbers of woodsmen and trappers claim to have seen the ghosts of the two lovers paddling a spectral white canoe on dark and silent nights when the quiet surface of Lake Drummond mirrors the blazing stars overhead.

That this was the legend Moore heard on his excursion to the swamp is evident from the following summary of the story, quoted from an anonymous source, that he used as a preface to his poem:

"They tell of a young man, who lost his mind upon the death of a girl he loved, and who, suddenly disappearing from his friends, was never afterwards heard of. As he had frequently said, in his ravings, that the girl was not dead, but had gone to the Dismal Swamp, it is supposed he had wandered into that dreary wilderness, and had died of hunger, or been lost in some of its dreadful morasses."

Moore's poem, based on the legend of the ghostly lovers of the Great Dismal Swamp, was first printed in his *Poems Relating to America,* published in London in 1806, and dedicated to "Francis, Earl of Moira, General of His Majesties Forces, Master General of the Ordnance, Constable of the Tower, etc." This is the poem, the only known Virginia ghost story ever to be immortalized by a poet of international reputation.

A BALLAD

THE LAKE OF THE DISMAL SWAMP.
WRITTEN AT NORFOLK, IN VIRGINIA.

"They made her a grave, too cold and damp
"For a soul so warm and true;
"And she's gone to the Lake of the Dismal Swamp,
"Where, all night long, by a fire-fly lamp,
"She paddles her white canoe.

"And her fire-fly lamp I soon shall see,
"And her paddle I soon shall hear;
"Long and loving our life shall be,
"And I'll hide the maid in a cypress tree,
"When the footstep of death is near."

Away to the Dismal Swamp he speeds—
His path was rugged and sore,
Through tangled juniper, beds of reeds,
Through many a fen, where the serpent feeds,
And man never trod before.

And, when on the earth he sunk to sleep,
If slumber his eyelids knew,
He lay, where the deadly vine doth weep
Its venomous tear and nightly steep
The flesh with blistering dew!

And near him the she-wolf stirr'd the brake,
And the copper-snake breath'd in his ear,
Till he starting cried, from his dream awake,
"Oh! when shall I see the dusky Lake,
"And the white canoe of my dear?"

He saw the Lake, and a meteor bright
Quick over its surface play'd—
"Welcome," he said, "my dear-one's light!"
And the dim shore echoed, for many a night,
The name of the death-cold maid.

Till he hollow'd a boat of the birchen bark,
Which carried him off from shore;
Far, far he followed the meteor spark,
The wind was high and the clouds were dark,
And the boat return'd no more.

But oft, from the Indian hunter's camp
This lover and maid so true
Are seen at the hour of midnight damp
To cross the Lake by a fire-fly lamp,
And paddle their white canoe!

A Mess O' Knockin'

The Poquoson area of York County, Virginia, that takes its name from the Algonquian Indian word "pocosin," meaning a swamp or dismal place, was the scene of a series of strange hauntings during the middle years of the nineteenth century.

Although only a few miles as the crow flies from Langley Air Force Base, the home of the ultramodern National Aeronautics and Space Administration, the place is still a remote and isolated pocket principally occupied by watermen and small farmers whose ancestors settled the flat and cheerless place during the early years of the Virginia colony.

At the time the supernatural occurrences took place, a man and his wife and their large family, many of whom have descendants now living, made up a close-knit community near the Poquoson River, a sluggish, marshy stream that empties into the Chesapeake Bay. On March 5, 1856, the mother of the clan looked out of a window and saw heavy clouds hovering over the lowlands that surrounded her home. Fearing that a wind and snow storm might prevent her from fetching in her cattle from the marshes later on, she begged her youngest daughter, a pert and wayward girl of fifteen, to help her drive the stock to a sheltered place. The girl, who was seated comfortably before an open fire, sassed her mother and refused to go. Flinging on a cloak, the woman went out into the bad weather to perform the task alone. When she did not return in a reasonable time a searching party was organized. But their efforts to find her were fruitless.

The next morning a fisherman pushing up Bell's Oyster Gut, a narrow estuary near the woman's home, discovered a bare leg sticking up from the marsh grasses. He raised the alarm. A party went to the place and recovered the missing woman's body. She had apparently lost her footing and had fallen into a pocket of quicksand. That she had put up a struggle was evident as the rushes and grasses around her corpse had been grabbed and pulled up in her desperate efforts to free herself.

The woman had been well liked. Everyone but the willful younger daughter mourned her death. Then eerie things began to happen, and the pert young miss had every reason to regret her unco-operative attitude as time went on.

Shortly after the funeral the girl went to visit nearby relations. She had not been there long before ghostly knockings began to echo loudly throughout the house. When someone, thinking it might be pranksters, grabbed up a heavy piece of wood and barred the door, the bar leaped into the air from its iron fastenings and flew across the room. While the knockings were at their worst, the man of the house, who was tying up his skiff in the nearby marsh, heard them a quarter of a mile away. Thinking it was caused by neighborhood children up to no good, he cut a hefty switch and sneaked homeward, hoping to surprise them. But on arriving he found his family and the young visitor cowering in terror as the knocks, "like an iron fist beating on a thin board," continued.

It was also at that time that everyone began to notice a strange reaction to the knockings on the part of the refractory girl. As the knockings became more persistent she would become increasingly hysterical until she finally fell down in a trance. When she recovered she would shudder when asked if she could recall what had happened to her while she was unconscious, her only answer being a wild-eyed affirmative shake of the head. But no amount of prodding could induce her to reveal what she had experienced. Then another episode in the strange saga took place.

The night the girl returned home from her hectic visit she went to bed early. Not long after, she fell into a death-like slumber, and the trundle bed on which she lay was lifted high into the air by unseen hands. No efforts of those present were able to return it to its place on the floor until the unseen power that had raised it decided to restore things to normal.

Hoping to thwart the evil force, one of the girl's sisters placed a large Bible under her head instead of a pillow, but moments later it was snatched out by a ghostly hand and flung against the wall.

From then on the thunderous knockings followed the girl everywhere she went. In no time her former waywardness became a thing of the past, and she began to show signs that whatever was out to punish her was definitely taking its toll. Everyone in the Poquoson area believed it was the spirit of the girl's mother punishing her for her disobedience, and one of her relatives is said to have remarked, "The old lady is sure riding that brazen gal's coattails."

Meanwhile, another strange manifestation took place. On that occasion the girl and a niece about her own age were sleeping in the same bed. When they awoke the next morning they discovered their long hair had been braided together in seven tightly plaited strands, while the knockings had been so persistent throughout the night that a man staying in the house told a friend, "I ain't had a wink o' sleep all night from that mess o' knockin'. There ain't been a minute's peace in that house since that gal came home."

By 1861, when the Civil War engulfed the Lower Virginia Peninsula like an all-destroying tidal wave, the knockings and other eerie phenomena connected with the tormented girl had become so well known that the Federal officer in charge of the Poquoson area took steps to investigate them. Hoping to get to the bottom of the matter and believing the strange noises and other eerie manifestations were caused by practical jokers, he had the girl's home searched from attic to cellar. That same night he went there to personally investigate anything unusual that might take place. In the meantime, to rule out outside human intervention, he placed a cordon of soldiers around the house with strict instructions that no one be permitted to enter or leave the premises. His efforts to solve the mystery were fruitless, for the knockings that night were so loud they could be heard for half a mile, while the lamp that was burning in the room where the officer sat was mysteriously lifted from a table and whisked through the air to a place on the end of the mantel. As a result, the baffled officer wrote a report of what had happened, ending with these words: "Whatever causes the disturbance is of supernatural origin, heard, but not seen."

A short time afterward another Federal officer's wife, who was a spirit medium, came to visit her husband at Fort Monroe. Learning of the strange goings-on at Poquoson from the officer who had tried to investigate them, she asked permission to hold a seance in the girl's home, specifying that the girl be present. The permission was granted and the meeting was attended by a large group of interested, but skeptical, people. It was a memorable occasion, for it was the only time the ghost of the dead mother materialized. What is more, she spoke!

After the party had assembled, they remained in a state of expectation while the medium concentrated intensely, hoping to communicate with the long-dead mother. Then the unexpected happened, for suddenly everyone was aware of a shadowy figure that seemed to be winding a ball of yarn as it stood near the medium. There was a breathless pause, and then the medium spoke.

"If you are the mother of the girl connected with these strange happenings, knit!" she commanded. And the nebulous figure began to knit.

Then, after another long pause, the medium spoke again: "If you are the mother of the girl connected with these strange knockings, groan!" And the wraith groaned loudly.

By then, everyone present was convinced, for the knockings had commenced with great urgency and the girl had lost consciousness and fallen forward, seemingly lifeless, in her chair. But that was not the end of the seance, for the medium gave one last order.

"If you are the mother of the girl who now sits here unconscious, speak!" And immediately the ghost called out the girl's first name, following it with a wild laugh.

That was too much for those present, and the room was cleared precipitously except for the medium, the girl, and a portly old Baptist deacon who had trouble rising from his chair but who sang out:

"Guide me, O thou great Jehovah,
Pilgrim through this barren land;
I am weak, but thou art mighty;
Hold me with thy powerful hand...."

But the hauntings had about run their course, for the bedeviled young girl died in 1869 and things returned to normal. Nevertheless, the excitement she kicked up in Poquoson caused such a stir that people there are still talking about it as though it were a current event.

Ghostly Tips

Oakridge on Hungary Town Road, about four miles from Nottoway Court House, Virginia, was the scene in the 1850s of two well-authenticated uncanny happenings.

The plantation house, famous for its beautiful mantels, paneling, and Chinese Chippendale staircase, was built during the eighteenth century by a man named Richard Smith, whose descendants lived there until 1842, when it was purchased by Captain Warner Wortham Guy. Born at Song Pleasant in Caroline County in 1797, Guy, who was twice married, lived at Oakridge from 1842 until his death in 1863.

Guy's heir, Colonel William Scott Guy, a son by his first marriage, who was present when the two strange happenings took place, told the story this way.

His father, one of the largest agriculturists in Nottoway County in his time, operated his four thousand-acre plantation on an extensive scale. In 1853 he bought a large supply of farm equipment from a firm in Richmond, Virginia, for which he paid cash. Unfortunately, the payment was not credited to his account, and after considerable controversy, he was told that he would either have to produce the receipt or pay the debt again.

Guy combed Oak Ridge from attic to cellar, but no receipt could be found. Finally, one day, as the time for the payment drew near, he lay down on a sofa in the parlor where his wife was sewing. A few minutes later he sat up suddenly and asked her if she had touched him on the shoulder. When she said she had not been near him, he replied, "Mary, that may be true, but I could swear someone just touched me on my shoulder and then told me to go and look in my bankbook."

When Mrs. Guy insisted that her husband had dreamed the episode, Guy lay down again, but not for long. Getting up the second time, he informed his wife that the experience had been repeated as soon as he had dozed off to sleep again. Mrs. Guy was impressed that time, and the two of them went to his desk in another room to examine his bankbook. When it was opened, the missing receipt, marked paid in full by the agricultural firm's bookkeeper, was discovered carefully folded and tucked away in a small pocket inside the back cover of the leather-bound bankbook.

Six years later, Guy had an excellent opportunity to make a very desirable investment if he could raise the necessary cash. Not wishing to borrow so large a sum and being temporarily short of funds, he tried to sell some stocks, among which were several hundred shares in the South Side Railway, in order to obtain the money.

Finding no takers, Guy had about given up hope of raising the sum when he lay down on the same sofa on a warm summer afternoon to take a nap. Dozing off, he felt the same touch on his shoulder again, after which he distinctly heard the identical voice that had previously led him to the discovery of the missing receipt, say, "Take the ten o'clock train." Waking up suddenly, Guy briefly caught a glimpse of a woman, wearing a sprigged muslin dress and a lace cap, that resembled his long-dead mother, standing by the square rosewood piano on the other side of the room. When he rubbed his eyes and looked again, however, the figure had vanished.

Getting up, Guy went to his family, who were sitting in the hall, and told them what had happened. When they all laughed and said he must have been dreaming, he went back and lay down again. In a few moments the same thing happened, and when Guy informed his family the experience had been repeated they recalled the episode of the missing receipt and urged him to take the ghostly advice.

As the ten o'clock train would not pass through Nottoway Court House until the next morning, Guy considered the matter at length, finally deciding to act on his family's advice. Bright and early the next morning he rode his horse to the station, made arrangements at a livery stable for it to be looked after for several days, and boarded the train when it arrived.

Meeting an old friend on board, he was talking with him when another man, a stranger to Guy, walked down the aisle in their direction. As Guy's friend was acquainted with the stranger, he introduced the two men. In the ensuing conversation the newly introduced man enquired casually if either Guy or his friend knew anyone who owned any South Side Railway stock, adding that he would like to buy it if the price was right and the owner could be induced to sell.

Guy lost no time in telling his new acquaintance that he owned a considerable number of shares, and when the man offered to pay cash for them, the deal was made.

After the transaction had been completed, Guy left the train at the next stop and took the first one back to Nottoway Court House.

George Washington's Vision

George Washington, noted for his stoical level-headedness, is the last American anyone would accuse of having been a visionary. If a story that was old even in 1856 is to be believed, however, the Father of Our Country had at least one memorable encounter with the spirit world.

Washington's supernatural experience first appeared in print in a Mormon publication in 1856. Twenty-four years later, a much more elaborate account of the same incident, based on an eighteenth century narrative by Anthony Sherman of Philadelphia, an acquaintance and former companion in arms of Washington, was printed in the December 1880 issue of *The National Tribune, A Monthly Journal devoted to the Soldiers, Sailors, and Pensioners of the United States, and the instruction of the Family Circle,* published in Washington, D. C.

The episode as recorded by Sherman, who claimed to have received it at first hand from Washington himself almost immediately after it had happened, reputedly took place when the discouraged General's half-starved and poorly-equipped army was encamped at Valley Forge during the bitter winter of 1777.

Shorn of the journalistic verbiage used by *The National Tribune* reporter, this is what is supposed to have happened.

Washington was seated alone one afternoon in his headquarters at Valley Forge preparing a dispatch when he felt a sudden uneasiness. Looking up, he saw "a singularly beautiful female figure" standing nearby. Overcome with astonishment, Washington was immediately aware that the surrounding atmosphere had become luminous and seemed to be charged with supernatural sensations. While he was endeavoring to take in the situation, he heard a mysterious voice say, "Son of the Republic, look and learn!"

At that moment Washington saw a dark, shadowy being, like an angel, floating in the air between Europe and America, that dipped water from the Atlantic Ocean in the hollow of each hand and sprinkled some on each continent. This action was followed by a dense cloud that met in mid-ocean and which moved westward, finally enveloping the American continent in its murky folds. Then, after much lightning and thunder, and the "smothered groans and cries of the American people," the cloud was drawn back like a giant theatrical curtain and Washington was shown a vision of a prosperous America stretching from the Atlantic to the Pacific.

Meanwhile the dark, shadowy angel turned his face southward, and Washington saw an ill-omened specter approaching America from Africa. This startling sight was followed by a frightful vision of fratricidal war that divided America for a time. In the meantime, another angel, whose crown was marked with the word "Union," appeared above the struggle bearing the American flag. Placing this between the divided nation, the angel cried out, "Remember, ye are brethren," and almost immediately "the inhabitants, casting from them their weapons became friends and united around the national standard."

So far, any student of American history will easily recognize the first two episodes of Washington's vision as symbolic representations of the American Revolution and the Civil War with overtones of the African slavery question. But Washington's supernatural experience did not end at that point, and no one living when the episode was published in *The National Tribune* in 1880 had any way of knowing what the third and most frightful part of the ghostly revelation might entail. Even today, with the twenty-four-hour-a-day specter of atomic annihilation that hovers in the back of the mind of any serious-minded person, the apocalyptic intensity of the last part of Washington's vision is frightful to contemplate. And only the words put into Washington's mouth by *The National Tribune* to describe the episode can do it justice.

"At this," Washington is reputed to have told Sherman, "the dark shadowy angel placed a trumpet to his mouth and blew three distinct blasts, and taking water from the ocean he sprinkled it upon Europe, Asia, and Africa. Then my eyes beheld a fearful scene. From each of these countries arose thick black clouds that were soon joined into one. And throughout this mass there gleamed a dark red light, by which I saw the hordes of armed men, who, moving with the cloud, marched by land and sailed by sea to America, which country was enveloped in the volume of the cloud. And I dimly saw these vast armies devastate the whole country and burn the villages, towns, and cities that I beheld springing up. As my ears listened to the thundering of the cannon, clashing of swords, and shouts and cries of millions in mortal combat, I again heard the mysterious voice saying: 'Son of the Republic, look and learn!'

"When the voice had ceased the dark shadowy angel placed the trumpet once more to his mouth, and blew a long powerful blast. Instantly a light as of a thousand suns, shown down from above me, and pierced and broke into fragments the dark cloud which enveloped America. At the same moment I saw the angel upon whose head still shone the word 'Union,' and who bore our national flag in one hand and a sword in the other, descend from Heaven attended by legions of bright spirits.

"These immediately joined the inhabitants of America, who, I perceived, were well nigh overcome, but who, immediately taking courage again, closed up their broken ranks and renewed the battle. Again, amid the fearful noise of the conflict, I heard the mysterious voice saying: 'Son of the Republic, look and learn!'

"As the voice ceased, the shadowy angel for the last time dipped water from the ocean and sprinkled it upon America. Instantly the dark cloud rolled back, together with the armies it had brought, leaving the land victorious.

"Then, once more, I beheld villages, towns, and cities springing up where they had been before, while the bright angel, planting the azure standard he had brought in the midst of them, cried out in a loud voice, 'While the stars remain and the heavens send down dew on the earth, so long shall the Republic last.' And taking from his brow the crown on which was blazoned the word 'Union,' he placed it upon the standard, while the people, kneeling down, said 'Amen.'

"The scene instantly began to fade and dissolve, and I at last saw nothing but the rising, curling vapor I had first beheld. This also disappearing, I found myself once more gazing on my mysterious visitor, who, in the same voice I heard before, said: 'Son of the Republic, what ye have seen is thus interpreted: Three perils will come to the Republic. The most fearful is the last, passing which the whole world united shall not be able to prevail against her. Let every child of the Republic learn to live for his God, his land, and the Union.'

"With these words," Washington concluded, "the vision vanished, and I started from my seat and felt that I had seen a vision wherein had been shown me the birth, progress, and destiny of the United States. In union she will have her strength, in disunion her destruction."

The Feathered Spirit

Ames Ridge, an eighteenth century brick plantation house in Accomack County, Virginia, was the scene of a strange, unearthly manifestation during the early years of the nineteenth century. At that time three children were living there with their father: Edward Ames, aged eleven; Alfred Ames, aged nine; and Elizabeth Ames, aged five. Their mother had died a year or so earlier.

The incident took place when the two boys were ill of malaria, a common disease at that time on the Virginia Eastern Shore because the marshy terrain there provided a natural breeding place for mosquitoes. The boys, neither of whom was considered very ill by the doctor who attended them, occupied separate beds in one of the two large second-story, dormer-windowed bedrooms of the old house that had been the home of the Ames family for several generations.

Both boys were very fond of the children's game of battledore and shuttlecock, played by two persons using a couple of flat wooden paddle-like bats and feathered cork shuttlecocks. As young Alfred Ames lay in the gathering twilight, he reflected on what great fun it would be when he and his brother Edward had recovered sufficiently to play their favorite game again on the green lawn of their home under the wide-spreading branches of the surrounding trees.

Then, quite suddenly, Alfred Ames realized that something strange was happening in the gradually darkening room. Glancing uneasily toward the bed on which his brother Edward had apparently been resting quietly, Alfred Ames distinctly saw something that resembled the white feathers of a shuttlecock rise from his brother's upturned face and drift upward slowly until it disappeared through the ceiling. Alarmed, but keeping this observation to himself, Alfred Ames called for help, and the subsequent investigation showed that his brother Edward had just died.

The eerie experience greatly disturbed Alfred Ames, but he never mentioned it to anyone, and only wrote down an account of it many years later on the anniversary of his brother's death, in his diary, which he kept under lock and key in a drawer of his desk at all times.

In the meantime, Alfred Ames grew up, attended Dickenson College in Pennsylvania, and eventually became one of the most prominent ministers in the Southern Methodist Church. His sister, Elizabeth Ames, married the Reverend Charles Hall, a nationally known Episcopal clergyman, who, in 1887, conducted the funeral of the Reverend Henry Ward Beecher, the brother of Mrs. Harriet Beecher Stowe of *Uncle Tom's Cabin* fame.

The Reverend Alfred Ames and his sister, Mrs. Hall, were very closely attached to one another, as is often the case of children who lose their parents at an early age. About three years before their death (they died within six days of each other) they were talking over the events of their childhood one evening, during which the tragic early death of their brother Edward was mentioned.

Suddenly Mrs. Hall leaned toward her brother, touched him gently, and said, "Alfred, I am going to tell you about an incident connected with Edward's death that I have never discussed with anyone."

Then, after a pause, she continued, "The night Edward died, I climbed the stairs as quietly as I could and opened the door to the bedroom in which you two were recovering from malaria. Just as I peered around the edge of the door into the room, I saw Edward's soul, looking like one of the shuttlecocks you used to play with, rise up slowly from his face and disappear through the ceiling."

The Reverend Alfred Ames was visibly moved by his sister's revelation and sat in stunned silence for some minutes. Then he went to his desk, unlocked a drawer, and got out his diary.

"Sister," he said, "I never knew until tonight that you were anywhere near that bedroom when Edward died, but I also saw the same thing you have just described."

After another long pause, he added, "It also disturbed me so badly that I never dared to mention it to anyone. But if you will look in my diary here on the page that I keep marked with a lock of Edward's hair wrapped in tissue paper, you will see that I finally had to write it down to relieve my mind."

A Ghostly Tapping Paid Off

During the early years of the twentieth century, when the Berkley section of Norfolk, Virginia, was one of the lumber capitals of the South, a middle-aged bachelor, who was employed as a lumber grader for one of the big mills on the Southern Branch of the Elizabeth River, lived with his widowed sister in a large, old-fashioned house near the railroad tracks on the outskirts of town.

A deeply religious man of strictly temperate habits, the man usually retired to his bedroom every night after supper to read his Bible until bedtime. Unfortunately, one day when he was walking along a chain of fast-moving flat cars loaded with great pine logs headed for the buzz saws, he lost his footing, fell under the rapidly-turning wheels and was killed instantly.

As he had never been known to squander his earnings, his sister, who was his only heir, had every reason to expect that he would have accumulated a good sum in cash or other securities. But although a thorough search of his effects was made and enquiries were lodged at the local bank and building and loan associations, nothing could be found.

A few months after her brother's sudden, tragic death his sister rented his former bedroom to two young men who had been hired in the meantime as bookkeepers by the same lumber company for which her brother had worked. All went well for the first few nights that they occupied the room. Then a mysterious tapping began to be heard each

evening around midnight, emanating from the closet that occupied one side of the bedroom fireplace.

Thinking at first that the noise was caused by rats or mice in the woodwork, the two young men ignored it. When it continued regularly at the same time each night, however, they realized that something out of the ordinary was at the bottom of the matter.

With this observation, they decided to investigate, hoping to discover some logical explanation for the mysterious nocturnal disturbance. Removing everything from the closet, they examined its back and side walls, ceiling and floorboards, but although the house was an old one, they could discover nothing that would indicate the sound was caused by rodents or loose plaster or woodwork jarred suddenly by a passing train or vehicle.

Then, almost immediately after they had replaced their suitcases and other possessions in the closet, the noise began again, only louder and more persistent than ever.

The next morning at breakfast the two baffled young men mentioned the occurrence to their landlady and asked if she was aware of it. But she only registered surprise, saying that her brother had occupied the room for years and had never complained of any disturbance. Annoyed at not being able to discover the cause of the eerie racket, which by that time was not only getting on their nerves but was disturbing their sleep, the young men began looking for another place to live. As nothing suitable was immediately available, however, they decided to remain where they were until such a time as they could discover another desirable boarding house.

Meanwhile, a few nights later, when the ghostly tapping became particularly urgent, one of the young men, who was undressing before going to bed, suddenly had a bright idea.

"Do you know," he said to his roommate, "we've looked into that closet from the outside any number of times, but we've never gotten inside and looked out into the room."

"God only knows what good that'll do," the other man replied, "but if you think it might help the situation there's no reason why we can't give it a try."

Placing the lighted kerosene lamp on the end of the mantel nearest the closet, the young men opened the door and dragged everything out into the room again. When the closet was empty they noticed that the shelf running across its top, obviously installed at a later date after the house had been built, could easily be removed if it was tilted at an angle. When this was done, one of the young men took the lamp and stepped into the closet and carefully examined the wall surrounding the inside of the door frame.

There was a moment of suspenseful silence. Then he suddenly exclaimed, "Well, I'll be damned!"

To his surprise, the young man discovered a small, regular, oblong opening in the plaster directly above the center of the inside door frame that had obviously been cut out with a keyhole saw. Reaching inside cautiously with his free hand, he felt something large and round. When he drew it out it proved to be a carefully rolled wad of greenbacks, tied tightly around the middle with an old shoestring.

Dressing hastily, the two young men summoned their landlady, and when the three of them had finished counting the currency, that was mostly in bills of large denominations, they discovered it amounted to a little over fifteen thousand dollars, the life savings of the dead lumber grader.

The two young men then presented the money to their landlady, after which they replaced the movable shelf and their personal belongings in the closet.

About a year later one of the young men married the landlady and got to use the money anyway. As for the mysterious nocturnal tapping, it ceased the night the bankroll was found and was never heard again.

The Prismatic Mist
Of Death

Because he was a man with only one story in his reper-
tory, Old Bill Etheridge, as he was known by his friends
and acquaintances, was snidely referred to by the town
smart alecks as the Ancient Mariner of Berkley. Far from
being offended, however, Old Bill reveled in the nickname,
for his one yarn, containing a remarkable supernatural
twist, was well worth an occasional ribbing.

Old Bill lived with his wife in a neat, white-painted
house on a side street of the Berkley section of Norfolk,
Virginia, until his death right after World War I. On any
good day of the year he could be found in the town's pocket
handkerchief-sized Confederate Memorial Park, where he
leaned on a cane made of a sawed-off billiard cue,
punctuating his observations on the time, tide, and the
weather with generous spurts of tobacco juice. Wearing an
old black felt hat cocked at a rakish angle over his right eye
and a baggy, worn, brown corduroy suit, the left lapel of
which always sported a big celluloid button bearing the
snappy motto, "To Hell With The Republican Party," Old
Bill occasionally strolled over to a battered cannon, the
park's principal ornament, and caressed it lovingly with a
calloused hand.

People liked to recall the time an old maid schoolteacher
from Boston, Massachusetts, who was visiting relatives in
Berkley, asked him primly if it had seen service in what she
referred to as "The War of the Rebellion."

"Hell yes, ma'am, if that's what I call The War Between the States," Old Bill had shot back. "What's more, ma'am, it made many a damned Yankee hop in its time."

But that is not the story that gained Old Bill his fame. This is how he told it:

"I was in the war right from the start," he'd always begin, fixing his hearer with the "steely eye" of the original Ancient Mariner, "but I came near not making it home after the Battle of Malvern Hill."

Then, after a pause, he'd launch into the story. "I got hit real bad in the shoulder with a Minié ball early in the scuffle and it knocked me out cold. I don't know how long I stayed that way, but the next thing I knew I was in a clean bed with a doctor peering down at me and a pretty gal standing nearby looking mighty sad. My arm ached like Hell, and I could hardly keep from yelling out, but after the doctor gave me something to ease the pain I dozed off.

"Instead of getting better, though, I got worse, and I was out of my head most of the time. But I still had lucid spells and I learned from listening that a farmer who lived near the battlefield had picked me up when he saw there was some life left in me and took me to his house, where he and his daughter, the pretty gal I mentioned, were looking after me.

"Well, as I said, I was so bad off it looked like the jig was up, and after hearing several people around my bed talking real serious about it one day, I lost consciousness completely. Then, all of a sudden, I was surprised to find myself alive and feeling chipper, and the funny thing about it was the part of me that felt alive and rarin' to go was standing next to the bed on which I could plainly see my regular body was resting. When I looked around, I saw three people in the room, the doctor, the old man who had taken me in, and his pretty daughter who was sitting next to the bed holding on to one of my hands and crying to beat the band.

"'Isn't there something you can do for him, doctor?' she asked.

"'I'm afraid not, my dear,' he told her. 'I've done about all I can, but the way things look now, I can't hold out much hope for him.'

"Well, sir, just about that time something told me to take a look over my left shoulder, and when I did I was staring right smack into a goldarned rainbow. Not the kind you seen in the sky after a summer storm, mind you, but a wide curtain of rainbow mist—red, blue, yellow, green, purple, pink—you name them, and they twinkled like the sun was shining on them. Then all of a sudden I saw something moving behind the mist, and when I peered closer I saw my father's mother, Old Granny Etheridge, who died when I was a little shaver, and my twin sister, Little Emmy, who also died of diphtheria when she was seven.

"Both of them smiled out of the mist at me and Granny beckoned to me to come and join her, but before I could do it, Little Emmy signaled to me to stay where I was. Then she said real solemn like, 'Billy, we'd love for you to come over here and keep us company, but I want to warn you before hand if you come through the mist, you won't ever be able to go back to where you are again.'

"Well, when she said that, I looked around and saw that pretty gal sitting there holding my hand and sobbing, and I made up my mind then and there to forget all about that rainbow curtain because I wanted to keep on living just to be with her.

"After that, I don't remember much about what went on for some time, but before long I was sitting up and that pretty gal looked better to me every day. Yes, sir, we really had a case, and I can tell you one of the hardest things I ever had to do was to tell her goodby when I was well enough to join my buddies again."

At that point, Old Bill would always make a long pause, after which he would add with an almost toothless grin, "But thank God, the war didn't hold on forever, and after I had gone through the rest of it without getting a scratch, I walked all the way from Appomattox Court House to Henrico County to see that gal again."

Then, rising to leave, for Old Bill had an excellent sense of timing, he'd always end his story this way:

"Now, buddy, if you've got any doubts about what I've been telling you, just come along home with me and I'll be happy to introduce you to my old lady—the pretty gal who made me want to forget all about that rainbow mist and keep on living."

Eerie Doings
At Clipp

When the events in this story took place, Jefferson County, West Virginia, was a part of Virginia. That, and the additional fact that the Reverend Alfred E. Smith, a former editor-in-chief of the *Baltimore Catholic Review,* once called it the "truest ghost story ever told," are sufficient reasons for sneaking it under the state line into a book of Virginia supernatural happenings.

The story began in 1790, when Adam Livingston, a man of Dutch descent, moved with his family from Lancaster, Pennsylvania, to the then-primitive outpost of Jefferson County. There he bought a seventy-acre farm near the town of Middleway, sometimes called Smithfield, and often called Clipp. Four years later a poor, middle-aged Irishman of respectable appearance knocked at Livingston's door and asked for a lodging. Shortly afterward the man, whose name was never known either by Livingston or his family, became ill. His host was a kind man and did everything he could for him, but it was soon evident that the stranger was not going to live. Realizing his end was near, the man told Livingston he was a Catholic and begged him to send for a priest to give him the last rites of the church. Livingston, who was a devout Lutheran and rabidly anti-Catholic, told the stranger bluntly that there were no priests in that area and if there had been one he would be reluctant to permit him in his house.

As a result, the man died unshriven a few days later,

and Livingston and his family prepared his body for burial. The night after the stranger's death Livingston asked a neighbor, John Foster, to come over to his place and help him "sit up with the corpse." When darkness fell several candles were brought into the room where the man's body had been placed in a crude coffin, but as soon as they were lighted they were immediately snuffed out by some unseen force. Even after they were relighted several times, the same thing happened.

This frightened Foster so badly that he told Livingston he would have to sit up with the corpse alone, after which he departed. Shortly afterward, Livingston and his family were surprised by the sudden racket of a herd of horses galloping wildly around the house. When they ran out into the moonlit yard to investigate, however, nothing could be discovered. But the sound of thundering horse hooves echoed off and on all night from Livingston's yard.

The next morning the stranger was buried and all went well for a short time. But the eerie happenings of the night before the stranger's funeral were only a prelude to the three months of horror that followed.

One week after the unknown stranger's death the barn burned to the ground. Soon Livingston's cattle, horses, and other stock sickened and died. Then the heads of the chickens and turkeys in his farmyard began to drop off in the most mysterious manner.

Meanwhile, the goings-on inside of Livingston's house were even worse. Showers of hot stones, appearing from nowhere, flew through the air, dishes and cooking utensils were tossed about by unseen hands, burning logs leaped from the fireplaces into the middle of the rooms, and heavy pieces of furniture were buffeted about like so many chips in a whirlpool. Added to these horrors, strange noises and frightful apparitions terrified Livingston and the rest of his family at night, while a large sum of money mysteriously disappeared from a locked chest in Livingston's bedroom.

Then a strange clipping noise, like the sound made by an invisible pair of giant tailor's shears, began, and in no time most of the family's clothing, counterpanes, blankets, sheets, and even high-topped leather boots were marred by crescent-like holes cut by indiscernible hands. This destruction was accompanied by an equally puzzling manifestation, apparently caused by a large unseen man's hand that burned its imprint, followed by the initials "I. H. S.," on any surface of cloth that might be exposed.

By that time, Livingston and his family were frantic

with fear and apprehension. He secretly enlisted the help of a local conjurer to put an end to the eerie disturbances, but the news leaked out. Soon hundreds of people began coming from long distances to witness the strange occurrences; some of them have left records of their experiences.

One woman who was wearing a very valuable Oriental shawl discovered as she left that it had been ruined by the ghostly unseen clippers. Another old Presbyterian lady from Winchester, Virginia, took the precaution of wrapping up her handsome new cap in her silk handkerchief before going into Livingston's house to satisfy her curiosity, only to find that it had been cut to ribbons when she opened the handkerchief again.

A skeptical man who wore his new swallowtail coat when he came to witness the disturbances and who was loud in his denunciations of what supposedly went on, came away with the tails of his coat snipped off, while three young men who drove a long way "to face the Devil himself if he was the author of these things" departed in haste when the hearthstone in the room where they were sitting arose from its place and whirled around the floor.

At that point, Livingston dreamed one night that he was struggling up a steep mountain. Upon reaching the top, he saw a man dressed in clerical robes and heard a voice cry out, "This is the man who can help you." The next morning he rode southward to Winchester to visit the Reverend Alexander Belmain, the Episcopal rector there. As the latter gave him little encouragement, however, he returned home. The strange hauntings continued without a letup.

Shortly after his unrewarding visit with the rector, Livingston had a talk with a man named Richard McSherry, a Catholic, who lived in nearby Leestown. McSherry told him that the Reverend Dennis Cahill, a Roman Catholic missionary priest, was expected to say mass in Leestown the next Sunday. By then Livingston's anti-Catholic prejudices were considerably abated, and on the appointed day, he, McSherry, and another Catholic named Minghini went to Leestown to hear mass. When Father Cahill walked into the sanctuary and began to speak Livingston became greatly agitated. Turning to McSherry, he whispered, "That is the man I saw in my dream!"

When mass was over, Livingston told Father Cahill his story. At first Father Cahill laughed and told him his neighbors were playing pranks on him. But when Livingston wept and persisted in his entreaties Father Cahill was so moved he agreed to go home with him.

Upon his arrival, he sprinkled the house with holy water, after which the ghostly manifestations, with the exception of the mysterious clipping noise, ceased. The next day, however, after Father Cahill said a mass for the repose of the stranger's soul in Livingston's parlor, even the clipping noises stopped, and all was normal again with one exception. When Father Cahill was about to depart, having one foot over the doorsill and the other in the hall, the sum of money that had disappeared from Livingston's chest early in the hauntings was suddenly deposited by unseen hands between the priest's feet.

Livingston and the rest of his family, with the exception of his wife, were so grateful for their deliverance from their three months of tribulation that they became Catholics. On February 21, 1802, Livingston deeded thirty-four acres of his farm, still known as Priest's Field, to the Catholic Church with the understanding that a chapel would be built there.

Later Livingston moved with his family to Bedford County, Pennsylvania, where he resided until his death in 1820. Over a hundred years later no chapel had yet been built on the land that he had deeded to the church. When his descendants tried to reclaim the land, the Catholic Diocese of Richmond finally took belated action and erected a small wooden chapel there in 1925. Since then mass has been said there every September.

The Ghost Wore A Tortoise Shell Comb

Mrs. Edward Peyson Terhune (1830-1922), the Virginia-born author who wrote under the name of Marion Harland, devoted an entire chapter in her delightful *The Story of My Life,* published in 1910, to what she called "Our True Family Ghost Story."

Mrs. Terhune, the mother of Albert Peyson Terhune who wrote the "Lassie" books, was Miss Mary Virginia Hawes before her marriage in 1856, and a daughter of Mr. and Mrs. Samuel Pierce Hawes. A native of Amelia County, Miss Hawes moved to Richmond with her parents in 1844, where the family occupied a handsome Federal period house at 506 Leigh Street, surrounded by an old-fashioned garden. No longer standing, the house was the headquarters of the Richmond branch of the Salvation Army before it was torn down several years ago.

This is Miss Hawes' story, supplemented by details not included in her autobiography from the reminiscences of other Richmonders of a bygone era.

An understanding of the first floor plan of the Hawes house is more or less necessary. The front door opened on a large, stairless reception hall flanked on the right by the drawing room and on the left by the dining room. Opening off the reception hall were two large arches, both of them outfitted with shuttered Venetian-doors. The one on the left led to a smaller hall containing the staircase to the second floor, while the one at the back opened on another smaller passage, to the left of which was Miss Hawes' parents' bedroom, while the room on the right was the bedroom Miss Hawes shared with her younger sister, Mea.

One winter night in the late 1840s Miss Hawes was entertaining a beau in the drawing room. He had brought along his flute and several new flute and piano duets, and the young couple had spent the evening sight reading them. When the young man left, Miss Hawes, who was known as Virginia in the family circle, locked the front door, took up a lamp, and went through the Venetian shuttered door at the back of the reception hall. Fastening its spring latch, she stopped by her parents' room to say good night. After they had discussed the new music she and her beau had been playing, she kissed her parents, took up her lamp again, and started across the small passage that divided the two first floor bedrooms.

At that moment, she saw a small, gray-clad woman wearing a high, richly-carved tortoise shell comb come out of her bedroom, glide noiselessly along the wall, and then disappear through the slats of the latched Venetian door into the reception hall beyond. Returning immediately to her parents' room, Miss Hawes placed her lamp unsteadily on a table, and said, "I have just seen a ghost."

This announcement obviously disturbed Miss Hawes' father, but he covered his uneasiness by trying to convince her that it had only been an illusion. Miss Hawes was not convinced, however, so her father not only searched the house from top to bottom to discover any intruder that might be hiding there, but also went with his frightened daughter to her bedroom to quiet her fears.

When Miss Hawes attended family prayers the next morning her father noticed her tired and apprehensive expression, and after breakfast he called her to one side and asked her to keep what she had seen to herself.

About a month later Miss Hawes and her father were talking in the drawing room one evening when her mother came in hurriedly and said, "I have just seen Virginia's ghost. I saw it in the same place and it went in the same direction. It was all in gray, but something white, like a turban, was wrapped around its head."

Miss Hawes noticed immediately that this fresh revelation greatly shocked her father, but his only comment was, "We will wait until further developments."

They were not long in coming, for a few weeks later Miss Hawes' sister Mea, her face as white as a sheet, burst in on her parents and herself. After closing the drawing room door hastily, she blurted out that something, presumably the ghost of a woman wearing high heel slippers that went "Tap! Tap! Tap!" had chased her downstairs. But when she looked back nothing was there, although the sounds continued behind her on the floorboards.

By then it was impossible to keep the secret any longer, and Mr. Hawes told the terrified girl what her mother and her sister Virginia had previously seen. He then implored her not to mention the episodes to the younger children or the servants.

Time passed, and nothing further happened until several months later when Miss Hawes' younger sister, Alice, and a visiting cousin were sent off to bed one night. As they passed the drawing room door and saw a glowing soft coal fire burning in the grate, they sneaked in and sat there talking and giggling until they heard the sentinel in nearby Capitol Square call out "Ten o'clock and all's well!" Not caring to be caught by their elders sitting up so late, they started to go upstairs. The Venetian-shuttered doorway opposite the drawing room door was open, and as a negligent servant had failed to light the hanging lamp in the reception hall, that area was dark. But the stair hall beyond was flooded with moonlight from an uncurtained window.

Just as the two little girls entered the dark reception hall they plainly saw a white-clad figure walk slowly down the stairway. Thinking it might be one of the younger boys in the family coming downstairs in his nightgown for a drink of water from a pitcher that was always kept on a table at the foot of the stairs, they held back for a moment, intending to surprise him when he had finished drinking. Meanwhile the figure descended the lower steps of the stairway and had about reached the place where the little girls were hiding when the front door burst open and all of the boys in the family romped in from an evening stroll.

At that point pandemonium took over, and quiet was not restored until Mr. Hawes appeared on the scene and ordered everyone off to bed. The next morning their father made the youngsters repeat their story, after which he tried to convince them that they had seen nothing. But Virginia was keenly aware that the accumulated hauntings of the past months worried her father more than he cared to show, and she was not at all surprised when she was asked quietly to join him, her mother, and her sister Mea in his bedroom. When they were there and the door had been securely closed, he spoke:

"My dears," he began, "I've called you in here to say that it is useless to deceive ourselves any longer that there isn't something strange about this house." Then, after a pause, he continued, "I've known it myself for over a year now; in fact we hadn't lived here long before I began having a strange recurring experience that has convinced me that unseen forces are at work here that I definitely don't understand."

When Virginia and her mother and sister requested the details, he began again: "Well, one windy November night I had gone to bed as usual before your mother had finished the book she was reading. It was stormy outside and I lay there with my eyes closed, listening to the rain beating against the windows and thinking over things I planned to do the next day. Then, all of a sudden, somebody touched my feet very gently. Hands were laid lightly on them, then they were lifted and came to rest on my knees, and so on up my body until they rested more heavily on my chest. At that moment I was also aware that whoever it was was looking into my face, and until then I thought it was your mother tucking in the covers to keep out the drafts. So when I felt she had bent over to look into my face, I opened my eyes to thank her. When I did, there was nobody there, and the pressure on my chest ceased the moment I opened my eyelids.

"Sensing immediately that something was amiss, I raised myself on my elbow and looked toward the fireplace where I saw your mother was still reading, her back toward me. I then turned over quietly and glanced under the bed, but all I saw was uninterrupted lamplight and firelight."

Mr. Hawes ceased speaking for a moment to allow what he had said to sink in, then he continued. "I am telling this experience now for the first time," he said, "for I have never mentioned it before, not even to your mother. But I can assure you that what I have described has happened to me fifty times and maybe more. In fact, it has happened so frequently that I've decided the hands that touch me are either those of a very small woman or those of a child. And when they reach my chest they always pause for a few seconds, after which, whatever it is that is doing the touching looks into my face. But when I open my eyes it is always gone."

After telling his experiences, Mr. Hawes made his wife and daughters promise to hold their tongues for fear that rumors that the house was haunted would depreciate its value. But these precautions didn't stop the little gray-clad lady from further manifestations, and on one occasion she is reputed to have helped rid the house of an unwanted guest, a sanctimonious old clerical relative who dropped in unexpectedly for what looked like a prolonged visit, but left precipitously the next morning for the home of another relative in the country.

Later the latter told Miss Hawes' parents the old codger said he was standing at his bedroom window in their house, looking out into the moonlight in the garden, when something came up behind him, took him by the elbows, and turned him around abruptly. He felt the two hands that grabbed him so plainly that he thought at first one of the Hawes boys had hidden under his bed and had jumped out to scare him. So he looked under the bed, in the wardrobe and closet, and under the washstand for the culprit. But nothing was found, and he declared afterward that he would not sleep in that room another night for a thousand dollars.

After her children were grown and her husband had died, Miss Hawes' mother sold the house in 1875 to St. Paul's Episcopal Church in Richmond. It was used as a church orphanage until 1919. But a change of ownership didn't faze the ghost in gray, for one of the orphans in later life recalled the "midnight alarms of screaming children at the vision of the little gray lady, walking between the double row of beds in the dormitory."

Then a discovery was made that partially explained the eerie visitations. During the time the house was used as an orphanage, the skeleton of a small woman was found by workmen in a shallow grave directly under the drawing room windows. There was no evidence that the woman had been buried in a cap or shroud, nor were there any remains of a coffin, a coffin plate, or metal coffin handles. But the workmen did make one significant discovery. Back of the small skull, they found a high, richly-carved tortoise shell comb.

The Butterfly Who Dreamed Of Death

Two prophetic dreams of Mrs. Julia Gardiner Tyler, the second wife of President John Tyler, have become a part of American supernatural folklore.

Born in 1820 on Gardiner's Island, her ancestral waterbound fiefdom at the eastern extremity of Long Island, New York, Mrs. Tyler was a daughter of Colonel David Gardiner, a wealthy international socialite and former United States Senator from New York.

One June 23, 1844, when she was twenty-four, she married the fifty-four-year-old President, who had recently lost his first wife. Julia Gardiner Tyler bore President Tyler seven children and outlived him by twenty-seven years. A giddy social butterfly in her youth and during her married life with President Tyler, Mrs. Tyler later became an ardent Roman Catholic convert. From then until her death she is reported to have prayed endlessly in her darkened bedroom beneath a blood-red hanging lamp shaped like the Sacred Heart.

Mrs. Tyler died on July 10, 1889, in the Exchange Hotel in Richmond, Virginia, in a room directly opposite the one in which her husband had died in 1862, and she is buried beside him in Hollywood Cemetery in Richmond.

In February 1844, when she was still single, Julia Gardiner, her father, and her sister Margaret, were invited by President Tyler to accompany him and a large party of notables and Washington socialites on a cruise down the

Potomac aboard the United States Ship *Princeton,* then the most advanced American naval vessel of her time. The night before the excursion, however, Julia Gardiner dreamed she was standing on the deck of a great warship and saw two skeletons riding two white horses in her direction. When they came closer and one of them looked toward her, she immediately recognized the gazing specter as her father.

Fearing that some tragedy was imminent, she begged her father the next morning to decline President Tyler's invitation, but she was eventually persuaded that her dream was only a figment of her imagination, after which she set out with her father and sister for the *Princeton.*

The party, enlivened by ample supplies of champagne, was enjoyed by all until the Peacemaker, one of the vessel's great guns, was fired. This caused such enthusiasm that a general request was made that it be fired again. Fortunately President Tyler, his future wife, and many of the other guests were below decks when the second firing took place, for the gun exploded, killing Mrs. Tyler's father, Secretary of the Navy and former Virginia Governor Thomas W. Gilmer, Secretary of State Abel P. Upshur, and so many others that the incident was proclaimed a national tragedy.

So much for Mrs. Tyler's first prophetic dream.

Eighteen years later, in 1862, when Tyler had just been elected to the newly formed Confederate House of Representatives in Richmond, Mrs. Tyler was at Sherwood Forest, the Tyler plantation home on the James River. She dreamed that her husband came to her bedside, deathly pale, holding his collar and tie in his hands, and said "Are you awake, darling? Come and hold my head."

The next morning the frantic Mrs. Tyler, accompanied by her infant daughter, Pearl, and her nurse, boarded a James River steamer for Richmond. Arriving there, she drove directly to the Exchange Hotel, where her husband was staying, fully expecting to find him ill. She was delighted to discover him in good health and spirits, however, and she decided to remain with him a few days.

The only room available was immediately over the hotel dining room, and Mrs. Tyler, the baby, and the nurse slept there that night. The next morning, shortly after Tyler went down to breakfast, Mrs. Tyler heard a sudden overturning of chairs in the dining room below, a commotion she later learned was caused when her husband had fainted as he arose from the breakfast table.

Tyler recovered temporarily. Refusing the assistance of

friends, he staggered upstairs, opened the door of his wife's bedroom and stood there, deathly pale, holding his collar and tie in his hands. Murmuring, "Come, darling, and hold my head," he collapsed on the floor.

Tyler lingered a few days and died just after midnight on January 18, 1862. Mrs. Tyler's second prophetic dream had been fulfilled.

The Quick
House Hauntings

If you light a candle in one of the upstairs bedrooms of the Quick House in Amherst County, Virginia, an unseen hand will immediately snuff it out. If you walk in the garden of the handsome white-trimmed brick mansion and listen carefully you are likely to hear a woman's hasty footsteps as she runs from a pergola in the yard to the house itself. These are the ghostly manifestations of a terrible tragedy that took place there over a century and a half ago.

When the house was built early in the nineteenth century by Edward James Hill, its extensive grounds ran down to the James River, while broad tobacco fields surrounded it on three sides. The house takes its present name from a family named Quick, one of its subsequent owners after the Hill family sold the plantation.

Many years prior to the Civil War it was the home of a man who was one of the most successful tobacco planters in Virginia. The man's wife, a very beautiful blonde, is still remembered for her fiendish temper and insanely jealous disposition, a reputation easily believed from the story that follows.

Tradition says the tobacco planter eventually grew tired of his wife's constant nagging and tempestuous rages and committed suicide. Her reputation as a scold did not stop the widow from looking around for another husband, however. Soon after her distracted mate had been buried in the family graveyard she tossed decorum to the wind and gave one splendid party after another in order to achieve her purpose.

In those days Rosemont Plantation, the home of the Landrum family, adjoined the widow's estate, and as young George Landrum, the weak but handsome eldest son and heir, had just returned home after graduating with honors at the University of Virginia, he was soon caught up in the constant round of the scheming widow's balls and dinner parties. Friends cautioned him concerning her evil disposition, but Landrum was so infatuated by her blonde loveliness and her superficial gaiety that he was soon ensnared. In order to remove him from temptation, his father sent him north to study law.

Meanwhile the widow visited New Orleans for Mardi Gras, and while there was attracted by a very beautiful young slave girl, supposedly an octoroon, who had been put up for sale on the slave block of the St. Louis Hotel. Fascinated by the delicacy of the girl's features and her fluency in French, the widow bought her and brought her back home to act as her lady's maid and companion. This move, the evil widow learned much to her chagrin, was the worst thing she could have done, for it was not long before people, particularly the men of the area, were making disparaging contrasts between her pale beauty and the dazzling loveliness of the slave girl. When this persisted, the widow wreaked her vengeance on the girl by whipping her severely on the slightest provocation.

Matters were brought to a head when George Landrum returned home for the Christmas holidays and attended a grand ball in the company of the widow, who brought her maid along as her attendant. Everyone noticed that Landrum admired the maid more than the mistress. And when the widow returned home she beat the poor girl unmercifully. Rumors spread by the widow's other servants soon got abroad, and it was not long before they reached George Landrum's ears.

Revolted at the cruelty attributed by gossip to the widow, Landrum rode over to her house one dark, stormy evening to remonstrate with her. When he reached the gate and dismounted he heard someone running down the path from the house. It was the slave girl. Flinging herself into his arms, the terrified girl cried out, *"Ah, c'est vous, Monsieur, pardon je vous prie."* Then, amazed at her boldness, she drew back, but not before the widow, who had followed her, saw what had happened. Giving Landrum a scornful look, she swept back into the house. After the slave girl followed her inside Landrum heard the sharp lash of a whip and the girl's cry echoing into the night.

Landrum avoided the widow for some time, but eventually her wiles were too much for him and he agreed to call on her when she promised an explanation. When he arrived he heard sobbing coming from a pergola in the yard. He investigated and found the slave girl there. Begging him to do something to mitigate her cruel fate, she remained too long in his company, and the widow again surprised them.

That time, when the slave girl re-entered the house the widow was waiting for her in the hall with a long, sharp butcher knife. Terrified for her life, the girl snatched up a pair of garden shears from a table and fled up the staircase to a second-floor bedroom, the door of which she hastily barricaded against the widow's attack. But the widow's rage gave her extra strength. With a snarl she pushed open the door violently and the resulting gust of wind extinguished the only candle burning in the room. It is this room in the Quick House where no candle can be lighted even today without extinguishing itself.

The sudden darkness added to the slave girl's terror, but for the time being she managed to elude the widow as the latter chased her around the room. Finally, when she was cornered, the slave girl struck out wildly with the garden shears and stabbed her pursuer, who fell to the floor screaming for help. This brought other servants on the run, and the slave girl hastened from the house and ran toward the gate.

In the meantime, George Landrum, sensing some evil was afoot, had ridden back to the widow's place. He heard the girl's story when she joined him at the gate. He pulled her up into the saddle in front of him and galloped off into the darkness.

But it was too late. The alarm had been raised by the servants. In no time a posse was formed to pursue Landrum and the girl. After they were overtaken, Landrum was brought back to his father's place and contemptuously dismissed. The girl was taken to the widow's house and was locked in the parlor to await the arrival of the officers of the law.

Realizing what her fate would be when they got there, for it was certain death for a slave to attack a master or mistress in the Virginia of that time, the terrified girl tore at the fastenings of one of the windows until she managed to get it open. Then, just as the sheriff and his men rode up to the house, she slipped to the ground and fled undetected through the high boxwood bushes toward the James River, ending up on a great rocky ledge that still projects over the fast-flowing stream.

Just then a man who was passing along the tow path of the old canal on the opposite side of the river saw a white form silhouetted against a dark background of pine trees. After a moment he heard a piercing scream, followed by a splash. Two days later the slave girl's body was found floating in an eddy below the river dam. But that is not the end of the story.

Weeks passed and the cruel widow had almost recovered from the stab wound when a carriage arrived at her home. It was occupied by a white-faced woman anxiously inquiring for the slave girl. This was her story:

Several years before, a young and indiscreet couple, each party belonging to a famous Louisiana family, had been the parents of a baby. In their efforts to conceal their indiscretion they handed over the child to a trusted mulatto slave to bring up as her own daughter. After the slave died the young girl had fallen into the hands of the slave trader who had put her up for sale on the block in the St. Louis Hotel.

Later the parents regretted their action and tried to find their daughter. Their search led them too late to the home of the wicked Virginia widow.

No Bye-Bye
To This Blackbird

As far as can be learned, Fredericksburg is the only city in Virginia that ever included a bird ghost in its supernatural annals.

The story, in which a sprite, reputedly in the guise of a big black crow, played a principal role, was far too mundane to have been immortalized by Edgar Allan Poe. It is a good deal funnier than Poe's celebrated Raven, however, which didn't do anything spectacular anyway but perch on a marble bust of Pallas and mutter "Nevermore!"

The tale concerns a crotchety early nineteenth century gentleman whose dilapidated home, near Fredericksburg's celebrated Federal Hill, occupied a desirable piece of property which a developer was constantly pressing him to sell. This the old fellow refused to do, for, being "set in his ways," as the old saying goes, he realized that if he gave up his home, his long-established habits would have to be drastically modified.

Over the years the old fellow had adopted a pleasant routine of dining each Wednesday evening with a lifelong friend, while on Sundays in good weather he crossed the Rappahannock River and had breakfast with a sister on her sunny front porch.

Apart from these to him daring ventures into the outside world, the old fellow remained at home the rest of the week. Eventually, however, he died, and immediately after the funeral the man who had wanted to buy his property made a deal with the heirs.

Bright and early the following Monday after the transaction had been consummated a crew of workmen arrived at the site with wrecking tools, but it was not long before they returned to the new owner of the property, threw down their pickaxes, and refused to continue the job.

When the owner asked for their reason, a spokesman for the group said, "Boss, no sooner had we raised the first pickax than a big black crow came flying out o' that house like a bat out o' Hell and began pecking at us so unmercifully we took to our heels."

This infuriated the new owner so badly that he grabbed his gun and made a bee line for the site. On the way, he met the sister with whom the old gentleman had been accustomed to eat his bacon and eggs and hot buttered Sally Lunn each Sunday morning. Recognizing the new owner, she told him an amazing tale.

"Do you know, the most peculiar thing happened yesterday," she said excitedly. "I heard something fluttering around on my front porch and when I went to investigate I found a big black crow perched on the back of the chair in which my brother usually sat when he was having breakfast with me."

When the new owner gaped incredulously, she added, "And do you know, he cocked his head on one side, watched me eat my meal, then gave me a rougish wink and flew back across the Rappahannock."

Somewhat taken aback, the new owner waited for a day or so, then picked up his gun again and headed for the old gentleman's late abode, prepared to settle the crow business once and for all.

That time he fell in with the friend with whom the old gentleman always dined each Wednesday.

"I'm glad to see you," the man said with a bow. "I really have quite a story to tell you."

Then, after a pause, during which the new owner eyed him suspiciously, he continued, "You remember my old friend whose property you recently bought. Well, last night was the first Wednesday evening we hadn't dined together in years, and I was feeling quite lonely and out of sorts, when suddenly something quite out of the ordinary took place."

By then the new owner was ready for anything, so he leaned on his gun and waited patiently for what he instinctively knew was coming.

"Yes," the old man continued, "just as I sat down to my

solitary meal, I heard a rush of wings and a big black crow flew into the dining room, perched on the back of the chair in which my old friend always sat when he dined with me, and kept me company until I finished my dessert. Then he gave me a knowing look, flirted his tail in the sassiest manner, and flew back out into the night."

Tradition seems to have forgotten the climax of the tale—whether the big black crow kept up its weekly routine, reducing the new owner of the property to continual frustration, or just vanished eventually into oblivion.

Sooner or later the crow must have gotten tired of bucking progress, however, for if you visit Fredericksburg today, you'll be shown the site of the old gentleman's former home on which a decidedly more recent structure now stands.

Grace Sherwood, Virginia's Super Witch

The History

Grace Sherwood, Virginia's most celebrated witch, has led a double life for almost three centuries. First, there is the Grace Sherwood of history, the only woman known to have been ducked for witchcraft in Virginia's long history Second, there is the Grace Sherwood of legend, the woman supposedly endowed with supernatural powers who made a trip to England and back to Virginia in one night to fetch rosemary to season her cooking, and who also reputedly tripped the light fantastic by moonlight with the Devil.

The historical Grace, who was born a few years after the middle of the seventeenth century in that part of Virginia known as the City of Virginia Beach, was apparently the only child of John White, a carpenter and small landowner. By 1680, when her father deeded land to her husband, Grace was married to James Sherwood, also a carpenter, by whom she had three sons, John, James, and Richard.

Grace's long and hectic career in court got off to a good start in 1697 when she and her husband sued a neighbor, Richard Capps, for defamation of character, an embroglio that was settled out of court. By September of the next year, however, Grace and James Sherwood were back before the justices with two suits for slander against two separate couples who lived in their neighborhood.

In the first, the Sherwoods said the defendants, John

and Jane Gisburne, had falsely claimed that Grace had cast a spell on their hogs and cotton crop. In the second suit filed against Anthony and Elizabeth Barnes, the Sherwoods told the justices that Elizabeth Barnes had spread a rumor that "the said Grace came to her one night and rid her and went out of the key hole or a crack in the door like a black Catt."

The case against the Gisburnes was thrown out of court. The case against Anthony and Elizabeth Barnes was also dismissed, but the Sherwoods were assessed for the costs and attendance of nine witnesses in their defense for the four days that the complaint was being aired before the justices.

Four years later, in 1701, James Sherwood died. Since he left no will, an inventory had to be made of what little estate he left. This document, listing such humble possessions as "one old bed & boulster & Pillowes & bedstead & a few old blankets being all of ye bedding" and "one poor mangy scabby horse" definitely indicated that the Sherwoods were not members of the gentry.

Four years after Grace had been left a widow she was again in court, that time bringing suit against Luke and Elizabeth Hill. Grace charged Elizabeth with having "assaulted, bruised, maimed, and barborously" beaten her because she had supposedly put a hex on Elizabeth. For this drubbing, Grace asked fifty pounds sterling damages, but the justices awarded her only twenty shillings.

Disgruntled with the verdict, the Hills retaliated by preferring a deliberate charge of witchcraft against Grace. Since she did not appear in court on the date appointed for the trial, however, the sheriff was ordered to "attach her body" to answer the charges at the next court. Later the justices ordered that Grace be searched by a jury of women for any tell-tale marks on her body that would indicate that she had entered into a compact with the Prince of Darkness.

On March 7, 1706, twelve jurywomen, headed by her old enemy Elizabeth Barnes, searched Grace for marks of the Devil and "found two things like titts with several other spotts" on her body. Since these marks, according to the general belief of the period, were supposedly the brands of the Devil imposed at the time of his consummation of a compact with a witch, it was apparent to the rank and file of Grace's neighbors that she had undoubtedly sold her soul to Old Harry.

Even then, the more enlightened justices hesitated to act, and as the county court had reached the limitations of its jurisdiction in the case, it used this loophole to refer the matter to the Royal Governor and Council and the Attorney General of the Virginia Colony in Williamsburg. Those worthies apparently had no desire to become involved in the case, for after deliberating the matter they passed the buck back to the Princess Anne County justices, suggesting "that the Court make further Enquiry into the matter."

With the case back in its lap, the county court ordered that the sheriff take Grace into his custody until she could give security for her appearance at the next court, and that he and the constables of the precinct in which Grace lived go to her house and "Search the sd Graces House and all Suspicious places Carefully for all Images and Such like things as may any way Strengthen the Suspicion." The sheriff was also enjoined to summon another "Able jury of Women" to examine Grace anew, but when the time for the trial came, the female jury failed to appear. The case was therefore postponed until the absenting jurywomen could be rounded up and dealt with, while Grace was enjoined "to be of Good behavior toward her Majestie (Queen Anne) and all her Leidge people in the meantime."

Since the sheriff was not able to impanel another female jury by the time the next court convened, it was ordered that Grace "by her own consent" should "be tried in the water by Ducking."

The day set for the ordeal by water was rainy, so it was postponed until July 10, 1706, at which time Grace was brought to a place on the Lynnhaven River, known to this day as Witch Duck Point, where she was stripped and bound in the customary manner, her right big toe being tied to her left thumb and her left big toe to her right thumb. Grace was then placed in a boat and the sheriff and his men rowed her out into the river to a place "above a man's Debth," where she was thrown into the water.

According to the curiously backward thinking of that time, if an accused witch managed to swim while tightly bound, she was guilty, but if she sank and drowned, she vindicated herself in a watery grave.

As the records plainly show that Grace swam "when therein and bound to Custom," that seemed to clinch the question of her guilt. She was therefore turned over to five ancient crones to be searched again for marks of the Devil, an examination that revealed that "she is not like them nor noe other woman that they know of, having two things like titts on her private parts of a Black Coller, being Blacker than the rest of her Body." With that knowledge in hand, the justices then ordered the sheriff to commit Grace "to the

Common Gaol of the County there to secure her by irons" until she could be brought to further trial.

No trial ever took place, however, for the well-preserved old records of Princess Anne County, Virginia, now the City of Virginia Beach, are completely silent concerning Grace until August 20, 1733, when she made her will. This was probated on October 1, 1740, at which time her eldest son, John, received her forty-acre farm, while her two other sons, James and Richard, received the sum of five shillings each.

Grace's worldly estate, including one "Inglish blanket," an iron pot, a pewter dish and basin, three low chairs, and "one frame table with a draw," plainly indicate she died a poor woman. So much for the Grace Sherwood of history.

The Legend

The legendary Grace Sherwood is a much more colorful character than her counterpart preserved in the old records. For even after more than three centuries have come and gone since the historical Grace was ducked in the Lynnhaven River on July 10, 1706, tall tales of her supposedly supernatural powers are still being passed down from one generation to another in that section of Tidewater Virginia where the actual Grace lived out her hectic lifespan.

Take the legend concerning Grace's ducking, for instance. Tradition says thousands of curious people came on foot, on horseback, and by boat to witness the event, and the crowd was so great that the shores of the Lynnhaven River in the area where the ducking took place were black with eager spectators.

According to this particular legend, Grace was slippery as an eel and managed to keep the sheriff and his men from tying her up until someone in the crowd suggested hanging a Bible around her neck. When that was done, Grace ceased to resist, and she was trussed up for the watery ordeal.

When the sheriff and his men put her into the boat and rowed her out into the river there wasn't a cloud in the sky and hundreds of birds were singing everywhere. Knowing that the Devil would revenge the indignity she was being subjected to, Grace yelled at the spectators, "All right, you hypocrites, you've come from hither and yon to see me ducked, but before you get home again my friend, the Old Boy will see to it that you get the ducking of your lives!"

As Grace spoke these words a sudden stillness permeated the air, followed shortly by the angry rumble of thunder from the northeast toward Cape Henry. When the spectators looked in that direction they saw a mass of dense black clouds boiling up over the horizon.

In the meantime, Grace was tossed into the Lynnhaven River and managed to swim despite the unnatural way in which she had been bound. Then, right after she was hauled into the boat again and brought ashore, the lightning began to flash, the thunder rumbled like the discharge of a hundred cannons, and the rain began to pour down in torrents.

Tradition says hundreds of people were washed into the roadside ditches and drowned trying to escape the fury of the storm, while the wild shrieks of Grace's mocking laughter could be easily heard over the deafening noise of the steady downpour.

Another story affirms that the justices could never keep Grace in jail while she was awaiting trial for witchcraft, for the Devil would come to visit her every night, loosen her fetters, and let her out of jail. Then the two of them would fly through the air to a point of land that still juts out into the Lynnhaven River, where they would dance wildly in the moonlight until the roosters in the area began to proclaim the dawn. The Devil would then conduct Grace back to her cell where she would remain until the next night's carouse. What is more, tradition adds that to this day nothing has ever grown on the spot where Grace tripped the light fantastic with Old Scratch.

There was also the time that Grace was supposedly tried and condemned for witchcraft in Currituck County, North Carolina, a few miles to the south of that part of Virginia where the historic Grace lived. Of course no record exists to substantiate this tale, but it is a good yarn anyway.

By the time the event reputedly took place, Grace had moved with her three sons to a place called Charity Church in the lower or southern area of Princess Anne County. It is there that Grace's grave is still pointed out to visitors. And according to a long-standing tradition the grave always remains green even during the heaviest snows.

To get on with the story, one day a crowd of men and women passed Grace's farm, saying they were bound for Currituck County for a frolic. Grace asked to be included in the party, and although the men were agreeable to her going along, the women were not, so she was left behind.

"All right," Grace called after them, "you all go along,

but I'm warnin' you I'll be there long before you get where you're headed for."

Thinking Grace was only bluffing to conceal her disappointment in not being included in the party, the group trudged on. Shortly after they had gotten into a boat to cross Currituck Sound, however, they spied an egg bobbing along on top of the waves, paying no attention to wind or tide. Several attempts were made by the men rowing the boat to break the egg with their oars, but each time it bounced out of reach and eluded the striker's efforts.

Then, just as the party was about to land on the beach, the egg washed ashore, broke in two, and out stepped Grace in her best Sunday-go-to-meeting clothes. Reaching into her apron pocket, she took out a long piece of thread, tied the egg shells to a nearby bayberry bush, laughed at the amazed boatload of people, and strolled away in the direction of Currituck County Court House.

When the indignant people caught up with her they preferred charges of witchcraft against her, and after a trial Grace was condemned to be hanged. Finally the day came for the execution and there was a huge crowd on hand to see Grace dispatched. But that didn't faze Grace.

"Look-a-here," she said to the sheriff in charge of the hanging, "do you want to see something you'll never see again?"

"Why, yes indeed," he replied.

"Well, tell that boy there to go to the tavern and bring me a couple of pewter plates that ain't never been touched by water," Grace demanded.

The boy did as he was told, but suspecting some devilment was afoot, he dipped the plates in the rain barrel and dried them carefully before he returned with them. That didn't fool Grace in the least. Taking the plates, she banged them over the boy's head and said, "Go back and get me two more plates, and don't dip them into the rain barrel!"

When the terrified boy had complied with her wishes, Grace turned to the sheriff and said, "Now if you want to see this wonderful thing, you'll have to take this halter from around my neck."

When that was done, Grace popped one plate under her right armpit and the other under her left one. Then letting out a wild, mocking laugh, she raised her arms and the astonished spectators saw a pair of gigantic bat wings had taken the place of the plates. Letting out a blood-curdling whoop, Grace flew up over the heads of the gaping crowd and sailed back home across Currituck Sound, where her tormentors found her upon their return a few days later, quietly smoking her pipe and hoeing her cotton.

People are also still telling the story of how Grace brought rosemary to Princess Anne County from England on a one-night excursion. According to this tale, Grace was cooking up a special meal for her three sons and their families and needed some rosemary to season one of the dishes. Frustrated at not being able to find any in the nearby fields, she took a long walk near the Lynnhaven River where she noticed that a tall sailing vessel had dropped her anchor opposite Lynnhaven Town. After consulting with her friend the Devil and learning that the captain and his crew had rowed ashore to get drunk at the tavern, Grace ferried herself out to the ship in an eggshell, where she found the cabin boy, the only member of the crew left aboard, sitting on a keg splicing rope. Hearing someone come over the side of the vessel, he looked up and was surprised to find a red-eyed woman standing there glaring at him.

"Boy," Grace commanded, "shake out the sails and hoist the anchor."

"I ain't got the strength to do it," the boy replied.

"You do what I tell you to do and not what you say you can't do," Grace shot back so fiercely the boy lost no time in obeying her orders. When he carried out her wishes, he found the sails unfurled and the anchor came up out of the river mud as if by magic.

At that point a strong wind began to blow and the ship moved out of Lynnhaven Inlet and headed eastward like a swift-winging gull, sailing so fast she reached England in a few hours. Grace then went ashore and got her rosemary plants, after which she caused the winds to reverse, and the ship made an equally rapid return voyage to Virginia.

The next morning when the captain and his crew came staggering aboard they found rosemary leaves strewn all over the deck. The cabin boy was discovered asleep in a bunk in the galley, and when they had shaken some sense into him, he had a wild tale to tell.

"A red-eyed witch woman came aboard last night and took the ship to Bristol and back," he explained. "She got a mess of rosemary, and I know I was there because I kissed my sweetheart goodbye on the dock before we made the return trip."

Even in death, the legendary Grace was true to character. They say a terrible storm was raging the night she died. Knowing that she didn't have long to live, Grace called her three sons to her bedside. Just then a sudden gust of wind howled down the chimney, scattering the few glowing embers that blinked there. Finally, when a tallow candle was lighted, Grace's sons were astonished to find that she had disappeared from her bed. In the ashes on the hearth, however, they discovered a distinct print of a large cloven hoof. The Devil had claimed his own!

The Specter
On Horseback

Dr. Daniel Conrad, the leading physician in the Winchester, Virginia, area during the early years of the nineteenth century, was, by temperament and training, one of the last persons anyone would have imagined would give credence to apparitions.

A son of well-to-do parents, Dr. Conrad received his medical training at the University of Edinburgh, Scotland, after which he returned to Winchester. There he not only built up a lucrative practice, but also lectured on anatomy and materia medica to prospective young doctors who sought him out because of his superior knowledge. Jovial and sociable by nature, Dr. Conrad was never happier than when he could spare a few hours from his busy rounds in the company of congenial friends. Toward the end of his life, however, he had little time for relaxation.

Early in 1804 the Winchester area was visited by a severe fever epidemic that continued each summer through 1806. Heavy rains fell every day from May through July each year, producing rank vegetation, while extreme hot and humid spells during the latter parts of the three successive summers greatly aggravated the distempers that in many cases were fatal.

During that period Dr. Conrad was almost continuously in the saddle in his efforts to minister to his patients, many of whom lived in remote areas outside Winchester. One of these was Miss Charlotte Norris, who lived with a brother on a plantation near Berryville, Virginia. Miss Norris had suffered for some time from what the doctor had diagnosed as a "lingering consumption," which he had more or less arrested before he was overwhelmed by the heavy case load brought on by the annual fever epidemic.

Feeling he had unjustly neglected Miss Norris because of his more pressing duties, Dr. Conrad set out on horseback one bright moonlit night around midnight to check on her condition. As a low-lying section of the main road he had to travel had been badly washed out by the constant rains, Dr. Conrad took at that point a narrow, parallel, higher road through the woods to keep his horse from being mired.

When he arrived at a fork that joined a higher and drier section of the main highway, he was almost thrown to the ground as his horse reared suddenly, whinnied wildly, and attempted to bolt in the opposite direction.

At first Dr. Conrad had no idea what had frightened his horse, and for the next few minutes he was busy trying to control the agitated animal. When he looked up, however, he was instantly confronted with the cause of the incident. There in the moonlit road directly in front of him Dr. Conrad saw Miss Charlotte Norris on horseback, dressed in what appeared to be a loose-flowing nightdress with her long, dark hair hanging down around her shoulders.

Incredulous, Dr. Conrad saw her smile and urgently beckon him to follow her. Then she turned and rode off quickly along the narrow side road through the open woods.

Dr. Conrad immediately reasoned that Miss Norris had escaped undetected from her brother's house in a delirious condition. He decided to make every effort to overtake her before she could come to harm. Knowing the tortuous woods path she had taken would eventually rejoin the main highway on which he was traveling, Dr. Conrad rode on. Meanwhile he continued to catch fleeting glimpses of the white-robed figure on horseback as it dashed along the higher parallel road in the same direction he was riding. When Dr. Conrad reached the place where the two roads merged again, however, he was astonished when the woman on horseback emerged from the woods, continued to smile at him for a moment, and then disappeared.

Baffled, Dr. Conrad reined in his still-trembling horse and took out his big open-faced gold watch. As it was bright moonlight, he had no trouble ascertaining that it was exactly half past one in the morning when the spectral rider vanished. Greatly alarmed, Dr. Conrad urged his horse onward, finally arriving at Miss Norris' home. He knocked loudly because of the lateness of the hour. The summons was answered by an obviously terrified Negro servant. When Dr. Conrad enquired concerning Miss Norris' condition, he was told she had died only a short time before his arrival—at half past one, to be exact.

The next day at a dinner party Dr. Conrad was teased by his guests because of his apparent lack of gaiety and high spirits. When he was pressed for an explanation, he recounted his early morning adventure. The recitation caused a good deal of skeptical laughter on the part of some of his friends, while other members of the party looked very grave.

The latter had every reason to shake their heads, for shortly after Dr. Conrad's moonlight rendezvous with Miss Charlotte Norris' ghost, he too died, a victim of the malignant summer fever he had done everything in his power to combat.

The Ghosts Of
Old House Woods

Old House Woods, a fifty-acre tract of pine forest skirting the Bay Shore Road near Diggs Post Office in Mathews County, is reputedly one of the most ghost-ridden areas in Virginia. Formerly the spot was open farmland, presided over by a steep-roofed, dormer-windowed dwelling with great brick chimneys at either end. Now the old house is gone and is remembered only by the name it bequeathed to the woods that took the place of the once fertile tobacco fields.

Today only two abandoned ramshackle farmhouses are within the precincts of the haunted area, and recently when three high school students "looking for some kicks" were exploring one of them they only found two things—a trapped sparrow beating its wings against a dirty windowpane and a battered paperback copy of Rex Stout's *Over My Dead Body.* The discovery of the latter was significant, for it would take a sleuth of the caliber of Nero Wolfe, Stout's celebrated sedentary, gourmet, orchid-fancying detective, to unravel the mysteries connected with the eerie place.

Tall tales have been told about Old House Woods for over three centuries, Mathews County people ascribing three reasons for its being haunted. One story says the crew of a pirate ship came ashore there some time during the seventeenth century, buried their treasure within the precincts of the present woods, and then returned to sea, only to be lost in a storm. Proponents of this theory maintain that the mysterious figures seen digging there on dark nights by the fitful light of tin lanterns are the ghosts of the long-dead pirates returning to reclaim their loot.

Still another story says two officers and four soldiers, all members of Lord Cornwallis' army trapped by the American and French forces at Yorktown in 1781, who were entrusted by their superiors with a huge amount of money and treasure, slipped through the enemy lines and headed northward, hoping to discover a British ship in the Chesapeake Bay that would help them carry off their booty. When they were followed by a unit of American cavalry, they first secreted their treasure on the site of Old House Woods, then made a last stand, during which all six were killed. As a result, some Mathews County folk say their ghosts still hover about the spot, guarding their treasure.

The third theory concerning the Old House Woods hauntings is the most picturesque. Following the defeat of Charles II at the Battle of Worcester in 1651 (his father, Charles I, having been beheaded three years earlier), the uncrowned king contemplated coming to Virginia, which had remained loyal to the Crown. With this plan in mind a group of Charles' followers sent several chests of money, plate, and jewels to Virginia by ship. Instead of going to Jamestown, however, the ship sailed up the Chesapeake Bay and anchored off what is now Old House Woods. There the treasure was landed. Before it could be completely hidden the king's men were attacked and murdered by a gang of renegade indentured servants. Manning the ship in an effort to escape, the bondsmen took only a part of the loot, hoping to come back and collect the rest later. Their plan was foiled, however, by a sudden storm in the bay, during which all hands on board were drowned when the ship capsized.

Those who believe this last story say the dark hour hauntings are caused by the ghosts of the royalist forces trying to guard the Merry Monarch's treasure and the evil spirits of the thwarted bondsmen trying to recover it.

Then there is the story of the "Storm Woman" who, according to a long-believed Mathews County tradition, dwells somewhere within the precincts of Old House Woods until towering black clouds over the Chesapeake Bay announce a coming gale. At those times this spectacular ghost, described by all who have seen it as "a wraith of a woman in a long nightgown, her long, fair hair flying back from her shoulders," rises from the woods above the sighing tops of the pine trees and wails loudly to warn watermen and fishermen to batten down their hatches until the storm blows over.

Many accounts of the hauntings in Old House Woods have been written over the years, but the most complete coverage appeared in *The Baltimore Sun* on September 26, 1926. Many first-hand interviews with Mathews County people of that time recount personal experiences, and it is from these ghostly anecdotes that most of the following stories are taken.

Although many strange things have been discovered in Old House Woods over the years, everyone agrees that the real treasure is still secreted there. Still another Mathews County tradition states that all attempts to dig for the buried hoard have met with tragedy and failure. Take the case of Tom Pipkin.

"One man, Tom Pipkin, a fisherman, who lived in the vicinity more than half a century ago," the *Sun* reported, "disappeared after a treasure hunting trip. His boat was found in the bay. Two gold coins of unknown age, and a battered silver cup, all covered with slime and mud, were found in Pipkin's boat. One coin bore a Roman head, and the letters 'IVVS' were distinguishable. No one would take Pipkin's boat as a gift, and it rotted away on Gwynn's Island. Pipkin never again was heard of."

That other supernatural forces are still maintaining their vigil at Old House Woods is also indicated by the following:

"A Richmond youth," the *Sun* stated, "had tire trouble at a lonely spot along the road near the haunted woods one night, very late. As he knelt in the road a voice behind him asked: 'Is this the king's highway? I've lost my ship.' When the youth turned to look he beheld a skeleton in armor within a few paces of him. Yelling like a maniac, the frightened autoist ran from the spot in terror and did not return for his car until next day."

But these stories pale by comparison with what follows, the first being a reminiscence of Jesse V. Hudgins, who ran a store in the town of Mathews Court House in 1926.

"Late one October night," Hudgins recalled in middle age, "our next door neighbor came over to our farmhouse and asked me to drive to Mathews for a doctor. One of his children was seriously ill. We had no telephone down here in those days. When a doctor. was needed there was no alternative but to drive to the village and get him. So I hitched up our horse and started for town.

"The night was windy and promised a storm before many hours. Scudding clouds concealed a half moon that hung low in the sky. But I could see well, and like any other light-hearted boy, I whistled as I drove along.

"Nearing the Old House itself, about fifty yards ahead of me I saw a light moving along the road in the direction I was going. My horse, usually afraid of nothing, cowered and trembled violently, and I felt vaguely uneasy myself. I had seen lights on the road before at night, but they always were a source of comfort and companionship. This one was different. There was something awesome and unearthly about it. The rays seemed to come from nowhere, and yet they moved with the bearer.

"I gained on the nocturnal traveler. And what I saw was a big man wearing a suit of armor. Over his shoulder was a gun, the muzzle of which looked like a fish horn. As he strode, or floated, along he made no more noise than a summer zephyr. My horse stopped dead still. I was so weak with terror and horror that gripped my very marrow, I couldn't even say 'Giddap.'

"I wasn't twenty feet from the thing, or whatever it was, when it, too, stopped and faced me. At the same instant the woods, about a hundred feet beyond the wayfarer, became alive with lights and moving forms. Some of them carried guns like the one borne by the man or thing on the road; others carried shovels of an outlandish type, while still others dug furiously near a dead pine tree.

"As my gaze returned to the first shadowy figure what I saw was not the man in armor but a skeleton, and every bone in it was visible through the iron armor as though it were made of glass. The skull, which seemed to be illuminated from within, grinned at me horribly. Then, raising aloft a sword, which I had not hitherto noticed, the awful specter started toward me menacingly. I could stand no more. Reason left me.

"When I came to it was broad daylight and I was lying upon my own bed. Members of my family said the horse had run away. They found me at the turn of the road beyond Old House Woods. 'You must have fallen asleep, and when old Tom reached the corner he turned too quickly and struck the fence,' they told me. Physically I was unhurt.

"The best proof that I had not fallen asleep was this: We could not even lead Tom by the Old House for months afterward. And to the day he died, whenever he approached the woods he would tremble violently and cower."

Then there was the testimony of Harry Forrest, a

farmer-fisherman, who lived within six hundred feet of Old House Woods.

"I've seen more strange things in there than I could relate in a whole day," Forrest told the *Sun* reporter. "I've seen armies of marching British redcoats; I've seen the 'Storm Woman' and heard her dismal wailings, and my mother and I have sat here all hours of the night and seen lights in that woods. We have sat here on our porch overlooking Chesapeake Bay and seen ships anchor off the beach and boats would put to shore, and bodies of men go to the woods. I would see lights over there and hear the sound of digging.

"Once I went out one brilliant November night to shoot black ducks. I found a flock asleep on a little inlet where the pine trees came down to the edge of the water. As I raised my gun to fire, instead of them being ducks I saw they were soldiers of the olden time. Headed by an officer, company after company of them formed and marched out of the water.

"Recovering from my astonishment and bewilderment, I ran to my skiff, tied up on the other side of the point. Arriving there, I found a man in uniform, his red coat showing briliantly in the bright moonlight, sitting upright and very rigid in the stern. I was scared, but mad, too. So I yelled to him 'Get out of that skiff or I'll shoot.'

" 'Shoot and the devil's curse to you and your traitor's breed,' he answered, and made as if to strike me with the sword he carried. Then I threw my gun on him and pulled. It didn't go off. I pulled the trigger again. No better result. I dropped the gun and ran for home, and I'm not ashamed to say I swam the creek in doing it, too."

Ghosts of human beings are not the only ones seen in and around Old House Woods. For instance, take the following harrowing tale.

"On one occasion a farmer's wife, living on a place adjacent to the haunted woods, went to a pasture to bring home their work horses. She drove them down a lane toward the barn. Arriving at the gate, she called to her husband to open it. He did not respond at once, and she opened the gate herself. As she did so her husband came out of the barn and laughed at her, saying he had put the horses in the stable two hours before.

" 'Don't be ridiculous,' said the woman.

"When she turned to let the team pass through the opened gate, instead of two horses standing there, she saw two headless black dogs scampering off toward Old House

Woods."

But the best story about the haunted woods concerns the ghost ship that has frequently been seen there. As recently as 1973, a fourteen-year-old Mathews County boy shared this experience with a reporter from the *Richmond Times-Dispatch.*

"It was two years ago during the summer. A friend of mine and I were taking a boat from Mathews Yacht Club over to Moon Post Office. You go up Stutts Creek and then over to Billups Creek. It was just after sunset and everything was sort of misty. Then about a half-mile from the mouth of the creek, we saw it. We both saw it, but couldn't believe it. I'd never seen anything like it before.

"There was a big sailing ship floating in the marsh. It had two or three masts and was made of wood. There's only a foot of water there but it looked like it was floating. It was the kind of ship the pirates used. We watched for about a hundred yards more and then it just disappeared. I went home and told my mother but she just laughed. She said everyone knew of the stories about the ghosts in the Old House Woods."

The best description of the ghost ship, however, was given by Ben Ferebee, a Negro fisherman, to the reporter for the *Baltimore Sun.* Ferebee lived near Old House Woods on the Chesapeake Bay shore. One experience with the spectral vessel was enough, he said, and after he and his family had encountered it, they moved to the city.

"One starry night," Ferebee recalled, "I was fishing off the mouth of White's Creek, well out in the bay. As the floodtide would not be set for some time, I concluded to get the good fishing and come home with the early moon. It must have been after midnight, when, as I turned to bait up a line in the stern of my boat, I saw a full-rigged ship in the bay, standing pretty well in. I was quite surprised, I tell you. Full-rigged ships were mighty scarce then. Besides that, I knew she was in for it if she kept that course.

"On the ship came, with lights at every masthead and spar, and I was plumb scared. 'They'll run me down and sink me,' I thought. I shouted to the sailors leaning over the rails forward, but they paid no heed to me. Just as I thought she would strike me, the helmsman put her hard aport and it passed so close that I was almost swamped by the wash.

"She was a beautiful ship, but different from any I had ever seen. There are no ships like her on any ocean. She made no noise at all. And when it had gone by the most beautiful harp and organ music I ever heard came back to me. The ship sailed right up to the beach and never stopped, but kept right on. Over the sandy beach she swept, floating through the air and up the Bay Shore Road, her keel about twenty feet from the ground. I could still hear the music. But I was scared out of my wits. I knew it was not a real ship—it was a ghost ship.

"Well, sir, I pulled up my anchor and started for home, up White's Creek. I could see that ship hanging over Old House Woods, just as though she were anchored in the sea. And running down to the woods was a rope ladder, lined with the forms of men carrying tools and other contraptions.

"When I got home my wife was up, but she had no supper for me. Instead, she and the children were praying. I knew what was the matter. Without uttering a word she pointed to Old House Woods, a look of terror on her face. She and the children had seen the ship standing over the woods. I didn't need to ask her. I began praying too."

Eerie Experience Resolved

One of the eeriest cases of extrasensory perception ever recorded in Virginia was experienced in January 1931 by two young men in Cabin Point, a straggling collection of old houses huddled around a general store in Surry County.

The house in which the episode took place, an early eighteenth century story-and-a-half, dormer-windowed dwelling, is still standing. Shortly before the peculiar experience took place it had been bought by the sister of one of the young men, the wife of a Northern university professor, with the intention of restoring it as a summer home. When her brother, a merchant seaman originally from Surry County, learned of the purchase, he requested its use for weekend visits as he was courting a Cabin Point girl at the time. The sister readily agreed to the arrangement, and when the young man decided to avail himself of his sister's permission, he invited one of his best friends from Norfolk, Virginia, to accompany him.

It was during the depth of the Great Depression and as money was scarce, the two friends hitchhiked from Norfolk to Cabin Point. Picking up the key to the house at the store, they bought a supply of groceries and kerosene for the lamps as there was then no electricity at Cabin Point, then walked to the old house which they discovered in an almost ruined condition.

Only one of the two first-floor rooms was habitable, and the young men spent the remainder of the afternoon making it comfortable. Building a fire in the rusty cast iron stove that had been installed in the bricked-up fireplace, they made up a couple of army cots with the bedding and blankets they had brought along, put away their clothing and supplies, then washed up and began to dress for a supper engagement at the home of the girl friend who lived nearby.

Although very few words had been exchanged by the two friends while these activities were going forward, it was soon apparent that both of them had experienced an identical eerie experience since entering the house. Consequently neither of them was surprised when one of them mentioned it.

"You're going to think I'm off my rocker," the young man from Norfolk said, "but ever since I've been in this room I've had the sensation of being watched by someone I can't see."

"That's funny," the friend replied, "I've had the same feeling, but I decided not to say anything about it."

Laughing and charging their mutual apprehensions to being in a strange place for the first time, they finished dressing and set out for their supper engagement. Around midnight they walked back to the old house through the darkness, poked up the fire, and turned in.

The young man from Norfolk went to sleep almost immediately and continued to sleep soundly for some time. About two hours later, however, he awoke suddenly. The fire had gone out, leaving a death-like chill in the room, and he was acutely aware that his friend, whose cot was on the other side of the room, was very restless.

"Anything the matter?" the young man from Norfolk called out in the darkness.

"No," his friend replied, "but I just can't go to sleep." Then, after a pause, he added, "I feel all kinds of unseen activities are going on here around me. Besides, I've got a screwy idea that this house is completely surrounded by a lot of restless horses and men."

"Oh, you just drank too much coffee at supper," his friend said with a drowsy laugh, after which he tucked his blankets tighter around him and went to sleep again. He then had a vivid dream that eventually served as a supplement to his friend's earlier strange impressions.

As he recalled it the next morning, he had the sensation

of being completely disembodied, and, in that state, he was conscious of standing in the room adjoining the one in which he and his friend were sleeping. Then he was aware that the room was flooded with moonlight from the uncurtained, small-paned windows, a fact that struck him as strange since he remembered it had been quite dark when he and his friend had walked back to the house earlier.

At that point he heard someone walk up the steps outside, cross the porch, then hesitate before entering the front door that opened into the adjoining room. Curious to know who it might be, the dreamer decided to investigate, and was surprised when he found that all he had to do was to wish and he automatically passed through the closed connecting door.

Once inside the other room he was again surprised that, although it was the same room in which he had gone to bed, it was also strangely different. The stove and other shabby furnishings were gone, and in their place a flickering log fire in the fireplace cast fitful shadows on several pieces of heavy furniture that stood close to the walls. In front of the fireplace was a round table on which papers, an inkstand, and several quill pens were scattered, while a lighted candle in a tall brass candlestick guttered on the tall mantel shelf. Further observation also revealed several pieces of eighteenth century men's clothing scattered about as though they had been abandoned hastily, while a large military drum stood beneath a window through which he saw the full moon, its broad silver surface interlaced with bare branches of leafless trees.

While he was taking in these details he heard someone turn a key in the heavy box lock on the front door, and when it swung open a small, elderly woman with a stoop, dressed in white with a dark shawl thrown over her head, walked in. Shaking out the shawl, the woman hung it on one of the pegs that projected from the inside of the door, walked over to the table and straightened the objects scattered on it, picked up the pieces of men's clothing and piled them on a chest, then drew up a low chair before the fireplace. Sitting down wearily, she buried her face in her hands and began to weep.

Overcome with pity, the dreamer floated across the room and paused beside the weeping woman, but said nothing. Finally, she looked up, and after regarding him for a few moments, she spoke. "Please go away and let me be," she said pleadingly. When he didn't move, she got up, walked to the window next to the fireplace, and looked out into the moonlit yard for some time.

After a long silence, she turned and continued, "They came tonight, you know, and he went away with them." Then after a pause, she added, "He didn't have to go, and I didn't want him to, but he went anyway...."

Then the dream faded, but it was so vivid the young man from Norfolk had no trouble recalling it at breakfast the next morning. After that, he put it out of his mind as something that couldn't be explained. But he was wrong.

A few days later when the two friends were hitchhiking back to Norfolk, they stopped in a cafe in Surry Court House and ordered breakfast. While it was being prepared, a man entered the place and was instantly recognized by the young man from Surry County as an authority on the early history of that area.

Striking up a conversation, but intentionally neglecting to mention his Norfolk friend's strange dream or his equally eerie sensations, he asked the man if he knew anything remarkable about the old house at Cabin Point his sister had just bought.

"Indeed I do," the man replied. "It was used late one night in January 1781 by the Baron von Steuben as his headquarters when he raised the Surry militia to protect the county from Benedict Arnold, who was then moving up the James River from Portsmouth for an attack on Richmond."

Then, after a pause, he added, "You won't be interested in the man who lived there at that time, but he was a real hero nevertheless. He was old and had fought in the French and Indian War and didn't have to go along with Von Steuben because of his age. But he went anyway and was killed in a skirmish with the British a few months later."

The Built-In Carpenter

Virginius Dabney (1834-1895), the grandfather of the Pulitzer-Prize-winning *Richmond Times-Dispatch* editor of the same name, was one of the principals in an uncanny experience that happened shortly after the Civil War.

Born at Elmington, his father's plantation in Gloucester County, Virginia, Dabney attended the University of Virginia and traveled in Europe before practicing law in Memphis, Tennessee. Having returned to Virginia shortly before the Civil War, he served in the Confederate Army for four years, mustering out as a captain. Dabney then founded the Loudoun School in Middleburg, Virginia, conducted preparatory schools in Princeton, New Jersey, and New York City, and later was associated with a newspaper called the *New York Commercial Advertiser*.

His chief claim to fame, however, is his novel, *The Story of Don Miff,* which depicts with charm and humor the life of the Virginia slave-owning class before the Civil War, a book that went through four editions in six months.

Shortly after mustering out of the Confederate Army, Dabney and a friend were visiting an old place in Loudoun County, Virginia, where they occupied a small house in the yard, the two rooms of which opened on a narrow hall with a door leading outside at each end.

Dabney's friend went away on a visit for a few days, leaving him the sole occupant of the small house. At first all went well. Then one night around midnight Dabney was awakened when the south door of the hall outside his room was violently thrown open, after which someone or something ran noisily along the dark passage to the north door, wrenched it open, and apparently fled into the yard.

Surmising it was an inconsiderate or drunken servant taking a short cut to the quarters, Dabney disregarded the ruckus, although it continued nightly in an increasingly noisy manner. Finally the disturbance got on Dabney's nerves, and he barred the two doors leading into the yard to prevent further intrusions. Nevertheless, the midnight visitation continued that night at the usual time, and although Dabney conducted a careful investigation, he could find no explanation for the disturbance.

Hoping to catch the culprit, Dabney sat up the next night, and when the racket commenced he grabbed a lighted kerosene lamp he had provided for the emergency, should it occur, and ran out into the hall. Although the footsteps and the slamming of both doors (still barred, by the way) were only too audible, he could discover nothing to explain the mystery.

This was deepened a few nights later after a heavy snowfall. Thinking he would discover wet footprints along the hall when the noise occurred, Dabney peered out of his room when it began, only to find there were no telltale marks on the floorboards although the racket that night was louder than usual.

When his friend returned Dabney told him what had been taking place, and the two decided to try to solve the mystery once and for all, if indeed it could be solved. That night at midnight when the door-banging and heavy footsteps began, they rushed out of the house into the yard, hoping to nab the prankster. But no one could be found, although the yard was white with moonlight.

Baffled, Dabney and his friend asked their host the next morning at breakfast if he had ever heard the strange noise. After an embarrassing silence, he assured them that he, and many other members of his family, had heard it many times. When they asked for an explanation, he said that when the small house was built as a plantation office during the early part of the nineteenth century, the carpenter and his father's overseer had been drinking heavily late one evening. A violent quarrel broke out between them and during the ensuing altercation the overseer grabbed up a pistol and shot the carpenter several times.

Realizing he was mortally wounded, the carpenter ran into the small house where Dabney and his friend had been staying, staggered down the narrow hall, and dropped dead just outside the north door.

The Ghost In
The Back Parlor

The yellow fever epidemic that caused the death of over two thousand persons in Norfolk, Virginia, in 1855 was also responsible for one of Virginia's best authenticated ghost stories.

The larvae of the deadly fever-transmitting mosquito, the Aedes aegypti, were brought into Norfolk harbor on June 7, 1855, in the hold of the *Ben Franklin*, a steamer en route to New York City from St. Thomas in the Virgin Islands where the fever was then raging. The ship had put into Norfolk because of engine trouble. When the bad news from St. Thomas was learned by the civic authorities, she was permitted to proceed to a Norfolk area shipyard only on the condition that "her hold should not be broken open."

After tying up at the shipyard dock, however, the captain violated his agreement. The hatches were opened and the bilges, swarming with the larvae of the deadly mosquitoes, were pumped out. Humid, rainy summer weather did the rest, and in no time "The Death Storm," as the pestilence was referred to by its contemporaries, was raging.

Those who could afford to flee during the early stages of the epidemic did so, but soon the debilitating sickness had reached such alarming proportions that practically every city, town, and community in Virginia refused to receive fugitives from the contaminated area. From then on, until the first heavy frosts killed off the mosquitoes, the Norfolk area was a death trap, the misery being alleviated only by the assistance of doctors and nurses who came to the stricken area from other parts of the United States.

One of these was Dr. Richard Blow, who arrived in Norfolk from Tower Hill, his home in Sussex County, Virginia, to volunteer his services almost immediately after the outbreak of the fever. Dr. Blow had two sisters, Mrs. George Blacknall and Mrs. Nimrod Hunter, who lived in a handsome Greek Revival double house on Bute Street in Norfolk that was torn down only a few years ago to make way for a parking lot. The house had been built for them as a wedding present by their father, who had thoughtfully instructed the architect to include a door connecting the first floor back parlors in the plan to facilitate easy visiting between the two sisters.

Dr. Blow, who had studied medicine in Philadelphia and Paris, came to Norfolk an embittered man. Disappointed when he had been refused a commission in the Navy, and having also lost two wives in close succession, he was more or less at his wits' end. Dedication he did not lack, however, and when he learned that his two sisters planned to flee with their families to their father's plantation in Sussex County to escape almost certain death from the yellow fever epidemic, he had no trouble in persuading them to permit him to utilize their big double house as a temporary hospital.

Dr. Blow was tireless in his efforts to alleviate the suffering he saw about him, but his ministrations were cut short abruptly on September 20, 1855, when he died of yellow fever in the back parlor of Mrs. Blacknall's side of the double house.

After the fever had abated, Mrs. Blacknall and Mrs. Hunter and their families returned to Norfolk, where they continued to live until their deaths. The house was inherited in 1900 by two of Mrs. Blacknall's daughters, who, finding it too large for their convenience, rented out the property and moved into an apartment.

The woman who rented their mother's side of the house, an outsider who knew nothing of Norfolk's history, ran what was then known as a "genteel boarding house." Because she used the former first floor back parlor in which Dr. Blow had died as her bedroom, she was careful to see that the connecting door to the other side of the double house was securely locked at all times.

Right after World War I when the Blacknall sisters sold the house, the woman who had run the boarding house for nineteen years called on them to thank them for their many courtesies while she had been their tenant. Then she told them a strange story.

On September 20 of the first year she lived there, she said, she was about to turn off the gas jet in her bedroom before retiring when she suddenly realized someone else was in the room. Looking toward the connecting doorway she saw a sad-faced, portly, middle-aged man dressed in black standing there toying with his gold watch chain. Fearing that someone had unlocked the door between the two houses, she cried out, only to see the man slowly disappear into thin air. From then on, she added, the same apparition had appeared every September 20 at the same time and in the same location.

This was news to the Misses Blacknall, who had never seen anything of the sort in all the years they had lived in the house. And when the woman assured them she was positive that she could identify the spectral visitor, they brought out miniatures and daguerreotypes of the long-dead male members of their family to see if she could link one of them with the apparition.

None of these answered the woman's description, however. She was about to leave with the mystery unsolved when one of the sisters suddenly remembered a miniature of the dead doctor that hung in her bedroom. When it was produced, the woman gave it one look, then cried out excitedly, "That is the man!"

It was Dr. Richard Blow, who had died of yellow fever in the room with the connecting door on September 20, 1855.

Assurance
From Beyond

Throughout most of his adult life Chief Justice John Marshall (1755-1835), the eldest of the fifteen children of Thomas and Mary Randolph Keith Marshall, wore an amethyst seal ring engraved with the words *Veritas Vincit* (Truth Conquers), the motto of his mother's family.

The Keiths had been hereditary Great Marischals of Scotland since 1010, when Robert Keith, the chief justice's remote ancestor, had been invested with that honor by King Malcolm II of Scotland. It is also from the traditions of the Keith family that one of Virginia's most fascinating ghost stories is derived.

Chief Justice Marshall's maternal grandfather was the Reverend James Keith, who was born in Scotland in 1699 and died in Virginia in 1757. His wife, Mary Isham Randolph, was the youngest daughter of Thomas and Judith Fleming Randolph and a granddaughter of William and Mary Isham Randolph of Turkey Island, the prolific pair that genealogists frequently refer to as the "Adam and Eve of Virginia" because of their many and distinguished descendants.

Although intended by his parents for the church, Chief Justice Marshall's grandfather became embroiled during his youth in an early Jacobite effort to restore the Old Pretender to the British throne. When the attempt failed, Keith fled to Virginia where he remained until he returned to England in the 1720s to take holy orders. Receiving the

127

King's Bounty for Virginia on March 4, 1729, he sailed for Virginia again, where he became the minister of Henrico Parish. Later he was the minister of Hamilton Parish, where he remained until his death, at which time he was buried beneath the altar of Elk Run Church, a building that has long since disappeared. All of which brings us to the ghost story.

During the Reverend Mr. Keith's younger and more reckless days in Scotland he and a fellow student named William Frazier entertained serious doubts concerning the validity of the Christian religion and the survival of the soul after death. At length their discussions ended in a compact (according to tradition written and signed in their own blood) in which they agreed that the first who died would, if possible, return to earth and report concerning the truth of these matters.

After the agreement was made, William Frazier shipped out to India as a military man, while Keith eventually took orders and became a parson of an Anglican parish in Virginia. Meanwhile years passed and Keith and Frazier lost contact with one another.

Six months before the Grim Reaper caught up with the Reverend Mr. Keith, a Scotswoman named Mrs. McLeod, who attended to the parson's dairy, was going quietly about her duties one evening when she felt a sudden strange chill in the room. Looking up she plainly saw the ghost of a man, dressed in scarlet British regimentals, standing nearby. Mrs. McLeod was considerably startled, but before she could cry out the apparition spoke.

"I am the spirit of William Frazier, who has just died in India of cholera," it announced solemnly. Then, after a brief pause, it continued: "Your master, James Keith, and I signed a compact many years ago when we were young men in Scotland in which we faithfully promised that the first one who died would return, if possible, and reveal if there is such a thing as life after death, and also if the Christian religion is true."

Mrs. McLeod was so frightened by these remarks she was unable to speak. After a long pause the ghost continued, that time more urgently.

"I can assure you that both are true," it announced with conviction, "and it is my desire that you go immediately to your master and tell him what I have said. It is also my desire that you inform him that he will follow me in death within the year." Then the ghost vanished.

Fearing to convey such an alarming message to her

master, Mrs. McLeod decided to say nothing concerning the matter to anyone. But the next night, as she was going about her duties in the dairy, the ghost of William Frazier appeared suddenly before her again, surrounded by an unearthly light, and threatened to do her harm if she did not deliver the message immediately.

Losing no time, Mrs. McLeod ran into the parson's parlor and blurted out the story. There was a sudden ominous silence, during which amazed looks were exchanged by members of the family who were seated around the fireside. Then the Reverend Mr. Keith, who was obviously shaken by the message, addressed Mrs. McLeod in a faltering voice.

"Undoubtedly what you have seen is the spirit of my old friend William Frazier," he said, "and from what he has told you I had better bestir myself and set my affairs in order." With that, he arose and left the room.

Six months later he was dead. His family did not rest, however, until enquiries made over a long period of time discovered that William Frazier had indeed died in India of cholera on the exact day his ghost had first appeared to Mrs. McLeod in Keith's dairy in Virginia. Meanwhile, it took more than a century before a final corroboration was put on the story.

In 1868, two of Mrs. McLeod's descendants who were then living in Baltimore, Maryland, went to Kentucky to confer with relatives of Chief Justice Marshall concerning a Scottish inheritance. And when the story of the appearance of William Frazier's ghost to their ancestress and the death of the Reverend Mr. Keith six months later was mentioned, Mrs. McLeod's descendants revealed that they possessed her Bible, in which, unbeknown to the Keith family at that time, she had written down a detailed account of the eerie events that foretold the parson's death.

The Queue
In The Fruit Jar

When the late L. Lee Barnes of Sedgefield Farm near New London in Campbell County, Virginia, decided to locate the grave of one of his ancestors, he little thought what eerie complications he would set in motion.

Barnes, who was born in 1887 in the big rambling old house at Sedgefield Farm, where he lived all his life, was a descendant of many prominent old Piedmont Virginia families. An amateur genealogist, he was constantly on the lookout for interesting data concerning his ancestors.

One of his distinguished forebears was William Lee, a brother of Captain Thomas Lee, who founded Leesville, also in Campbell County. On one of his genealogical pilgrimages Barnes visited the old Lee burying ground near his home in order to gather information from the tombstones there to fill out that particular branch of his family tree. Barnes discovered the grave marker of Mrs. William Lee, the wife of his ancestor, but none for her husband, a situation that perplexed him until he decided to do a little surreptitious digging in the immediate area of Mrs. Lee's grave to ascertain if his ancestor had also been buried in the same graveyard.

When Barnes informed his wife of his plan she objected strenuously. Barnes went ahead, however, secured the help of two Negro workmen with shovels, and proceeded the next morning to the old cemetery.

Barnes instructed the men to dig in a spot adjoining

Mrs. Lee's grave, and in no time what was left of William Lee was uncovered. It wasn't much, only a few small bones "and something that looked like a piece of rope," but which turned out upon closer examination to be a short length of tightly tied hair.

Barnes, whose knowledge concerning the dress and customs of former times was considerable, immediately recognized the rope-like fragment as William Lee's queue, an approved late eighteenth century style of gathering a man's long hair at the nape of the neck.

Collecting the few bone fragments and the queue, Barnes placed them in a large fruit jar, then had the two Negroes refill the grave. Taking the jar home, he showed it to his disapproving wife, then placed it on the mantel shelf in their living room.

Several days passed. Then one cold overcast morning, when Barnes and his wife were sitting around the big potbellied stove in their living room, they happened to look out of one of the windows into the yard at the same time. Both were startled when they saw a stately elderly woman, wearing a high white lace cap and a black dress and cloak, approach the window, peep furtively at them through a corner of the window, and then disappear into thin air.

Barnes went outside immediately to investigate, but could find no trace of the woman. Thinking it might have been a neighbor who had come to call but who had returned home because of some emergency, he walked over to her house, but was assured that she hadn't been outside all morning.

Almost immediately after this, curious things began to happen at the front door of Sedgefield Farm. The old brass knocker attached to an upper panel would rap loudly three times in quick succession, but when Barnes or his wife answered the summons there was never anyone there. As the knocker was a heavy one, Barnes was certain it could not have been lifted by sudden gusts of wind. Nevertheless, the knocking continued for several days, becoming more and more urgent.

By then Mrs. Barnes had come to believe that the mysterious visitor and the equally baffling knocks on the front door were in some way connected with what her husband had brought home from the Lee graveyard in a fruit jar. Even so, Barnes only pooh-poohed the idea.

Then the climax came in the form of a vivid nightmare. Barnes dreamed he awoke in his darkened bedroom in a state of great anxiety. A few moments later, the door opened and the stately elderly woman wearing the high white lace cap, black dress and cape, surrounded by an eerie light, walked in. Taking up a position at the foot of Barnes' bed, she pointed an accusing finger at him, and in commanding tones said, "Put it back where you got it!" Then she disappeared.

Barnes awoke in a cold sweat. Arousing his sleeping wife, he told her of the dream. Then, bright and early the next morning, he took the fruit jar off the living room mantel, went to the Lee burying ground, dug a deep hole next to Mrs. Lee's grave, and buried it. After that, everything was normal at Sedgefield Farm again.

Surry's Ghostly Castle

Bacon's Castle in Surry County, Virginia, now the property of the Association for the Preservation of Virginia Antiquities after three centuries of private ownership, has a long history of eerie hauntings.

Even today, after more than three hundred seasonal changes have come and gone, the old house is sound as the day the workmen finished it in the middle of the seventeenth century. And a view of it over the rolling Surry fields, with its steep A-shaped roof, its curvilinear gables, and its tall triple stacks of diamond-shaped chimneys, is a stirring link with Virginia's first century.

Built some time after 1655 for Arthur Allen (1602-1670), Bacon's Castle is the only "high" Jacobean house in the United States. Constructed of rose-colored brick, the fine old house stands in the midst of a magnificent grove of oaks and consists of two large, paneled first-floor rooms, two rooms on the second floor, and a lofty, dungeon-like attic on the third.

The Castle, originally known as "Allen's Brick House," takes its name from the fact that it was occupied for three months in 1676 during Bacon's Rebellion by seventy of Nathaniel Bacon's followers, who indulged in a good deal of "Ransacking & making what havoc they pleased within Dore & without." These depredations ceased on the night of December 27, 1676, when Bacon's henchmen, loaded down with plunder, fled from the house after its surrender had been demanded by Captain Robert Morris of the British merchantman *Young Prince,* anchored nearby in the James River.

So much for the Castle's historic background. Now for an excursion into its supernatural chronicles, a fairly consecutive account of which dates back to the time of Mrs. Charles Walker Warren, the mother of Walker Pegram Warren, the last private owner of the Castle, who died in 1972 at the age of eighty-six.

Mrs. Warren liked to tell of a visiting Baptist preacher who sat up late one night to read his Bible at the Castle when she was a young woman. The next morning he informed his hostess that he had heard someone come down the stairs from the second floor, open the parlor door, and walk by him. Looking up, he saw nobody, but at that point a red velvet-covered mahogany rocker beside the fireplace began to move backward and forward rapidly. Unperturbed, the preacher laid down his Bible and called out, "Get thee behind me Satan!" and the rocking stopped immediately.

Later another guest told Mrs. Warren she was awakened in the night by such horrible moaning and groaning from the attic above her bedroom she started to get up and alert' her hosts. After a while, however, the anguished sounds ceased and she went back to sleep. Mrs. Warren herself frequently told of hearing during the wee hours mysterious footsteps ascending and descending the time-worn stair treads of the Castle.

Still another of Mrs. Warren's stories told of a Negro maid, who, as was then the custom at the Castle, called to her one morning from the yard under her bedroom window, for the key of the locked house. A few minutes later, she informed her mistress that something amiss had happened in the downstairs parlor during the night. Mrs. Warren, who had been the last person in the room the night before and had left it in perfect order, found that a large nickel-plated reading lamp had been removed from the marble-topped center table and was leaning crazily against one of its carved legs. Although there were no traces of kerosene stains on the nearby upholstery or the carpet, the white glass lamp globe had been shattered into fragments. Mrs. Warren was also surprised to find a leather-bound Webster's unabridged dictionary had been flung on a sofa on the opposite side of the room from where it was usually kept, while its iron stand had been relegated to a corner on the other side of the fireplace.

But these eerie happenings pale before the real spook at the Castle, a mysterious, pulsating, red ball of fire that traditionally rises at irregular intervals at night from the graveyard of Old Lawne's Creek Church across the fields to the south of the Castle. The globular light, according to the many persons who have seen it over the years, rises thirty to forty feet in the air on dark nights and moves slowly northward in the direction of the former stronghold of Bacon's cohorts. After floating about the Castle grounds for some time, it moves southward again toward the ivy-covered walls of the ruins of Lawne's Creek Church and then disappears.

As recently as 1972, G. I. Price, then the caretaker of the Castle, gave the following vivid description of the mysterious nocturnal fireball in an interview with a reporter for *The Virginian-Pilot,* the morning newspaper of Norfolk, Virginia. Price, describing an experience with the light he had some fifteen years prior to the interview, said:

"I was standing, waiting in the evening for my wife to shut up the chickens, when a light about the size of a jack-me-lantern came out of the old loft door and went up a little...and traveled by, just floating along about forty feet in the air toward the direction of the old graveyard. I told Mr. Warren, who said he had never seen it, but his father and mother had, and if it ever came again, to call him no matter what time of day or night it was."

Skeptics strongly maintain that the eerie nocturnal fireball can be explained scientifically. The more credulous insist it is a manifestation of the Prince of Darkness.

One legend says that many years ago a shiftless, thieving servant on the plantation was late one night with his chores, and it was pitch dark when he started walking to his cabin in a corner of a field between the Castle and the ruins of the old church. The light appeared suddenly and the terrified Negro tried to flee from it. But it overtook him, burst, and covered him with a hellish mass of flames, burning him to death.

Another legend says an owner of the Castle saw the fireball blaze across the fields one night and enter his barn. Fearing that it would set the great quantity of hay stored there on fire, he ran to investigate. But the light took a sudden turn, emerged from the barn, and headed back to the churchyard.

Still another legend relates that a guest was almost frightened out of his wits one night when the pulsating red light sailed into his bedroom at the Castle, circled several times about his bed, and then retreated through the open window.

Another, and impossible, yarn states that a former slave on the estate averred the light was the soul of General Robert E. Lee hovering about the ancient mansion to ensure that any Yankees visiting in the neighborhood would not molest the Castle's occupants—all unreconstructed Southerners at that time, of course!

But the best tale concerning the mysterious fireball is the following.

A few years before World War II the light was glimpsed through an open window by a member of the Baptist church across the road from the Castle, where a revival meeting was in progress. When he called the attention of the other members of the congregation to what he saw, they suddenly became aware of the fiery sphere, throbbing with devilish brilliance in the nearby darkness. Tradition claims the mourner's bench at the church was rather crowded that night following the abrupt appearance of the flaming emanation.

Ghostly Chastisement

"I doubt if you'll consider this a Virginia ghost story since it happened in Ireland," the young priest said as he spooned sugar into his demitasse cup. "But since my family has lived here and has been telling it for three generations, I suppose you won't be stretching things too far to class it under the heading of Virginia folklore."

The priest was one of the guests at a dinner party in Norfolk, Virginia, where supernatural lore had been discussed. When he was pressed by his host to relate the story he had mentioned only in passing, he finished his coffee, then continued:

"My grandmother was the youngest of five children from County Cork, Ireland, whose parents died within a short time of one another around the middle of the nineteenth century. As the orphans had only one close relative, a very beautiful aunt who lived on a nearby estate, she assumed responsibility for them. Instead of being kind to them, however, she treated them barbarously.

"The two boys were forced to work in the fields with the farm laborers, and, if they stepped out of line, their aunt had them beaten by one of the farm hands. The three girls were employed as servants around the house, and, if they displeased their aunt in any manner, she would take them to an unfurnished room in the attic and whip them severely."

The priest paused for his coffee cup to be refilled, then continued: "This intolerable situation continued until several years later when the cruel aunt was preparing one night to attend a ball at a nearby estate. As her regular maid was indisposed, her three nieces were pressed into service to help her dress.

"Unfortunately my grandmother became so nervous at her aunt's constant nagging that she accidentally dropped a box of pins. As she stooped to pick them up, her aunt struck her a vicious blow on the back of her head with a hairbrush.

"At that moment an icy chill permeated the room. When the three girls and the cruel aunt looked up, they plainly saw the ghost of the children's mother standing near the dressing table.

"There was a moment of stunned silence, after which the evil aunt tried to conceal her terror by calling out loudly, 'And what is the meaning of this flummery, may I ask?'

"At first the ghost did not answer. Then moving closer to the startled aunt, it spoke: 'Why have you treated my children so inhumanely, when you should have given them the love that they deserved?' it demanded.

"Visibly shaken, but still brazen, the evil aunt laughed mockingly, only to be interrupted by the ghost of the dead sister.

" 'Don't try to put a saucy face on your devilment,' it said menacingly, 'for there is no escaping the punishment I have been permitted to come back to earth to inflict on you.'

"With those words, the sound of a sharp slap echoed through the room, after which the ghost vanished. Glancing at her face in the mirror the evil aunt was horrified to see that her left cheek was marked with a fiery print of a woman's hand.

"Frantically calling for soap and water, the cruel aunt tried to erase the telltale ghostly brand, but no amount of scrubbing could remove it, and she bore the mark until her death, covering the scar in the meantime with a heavy veil to conceal her shame."

There was a dramatic pause during which everyone at the table remained silent. Then the priest concluded the story.

"But the episode didn't have a tragic ending as far as the five children were concerned. The cruel aunt became so incensed every time she saw one of her dead sister's children she finally gave the eldest boy, who had reached his majority by then, sufficient funds to enable him to bring his brother and sisters to Virginia, where they settled in Lynchburg, and where their descendants have continued to tell the tale of the ghostly chastisement."

Blood On
The Millstone

One of the time-worn tombstones in the family burying ground at Warwick, the ancestral home of the Upshur family of Accomack County, Virginia, gives no indication of the macabre nightmare-predicted tragedy that it memorializes. The inscription reads: "In memory of Rachel the wife of Abel Upshur who died December 25th 1749 in the 47th year of her age."

Rachel, a daugher of John and Agnes Burton Revell, married Abel Upshur around 1725, and bore him five children before her tragic death. Rachel Upshur's husband, a grandson of Arthur Upshur, I, who had come to the Virginia Eastern Shore as a cabin boy from his native county of Essex, England, during the first half of the seventeenth century, was one of the leading Accomack County citizens of his time.

In 1738, after the death of his father, Abel Upshur, II, he and his wife moved to Warwick, one of the earliest brick houses still standing in Accomack County, where they lived the life of comfortably well-off Eastern Shore gentry of their time until fate put a period to their happiness one bitter winter evening in 1749.

Late that night, after the fires in the great fireplaces had been banked and everyone had gone to bed, Abel Upshur, who was ill at that time, was aroused from sleep by a wild squawking from the poultry house in the yard. The racket also awakened Rachel Upshur from a horrible nightmare in which a white-shrouded, grinning skeleton with upraised arms had solemnly warned her not to venture out of the house that night under any circumstances, predicting that she would meet death in some horrible unspecified manner if she disobeyed the admonition.

Trembling with fear, Rachel told her husband of the dreadful dream, but he ridiculed it, assuring her that it was not necessary for her to venture out into the night anyway. He then put on his clothes hastily and hurried out into the icy darkness to investigate the disturbance in the poultry house.

When he did not return for some time, Rachel, who was deeply concerned about his health, disregarded the prophetic dream warning. Getting out of bed, she threw a cloak over her nightdress and went out into the dark farmyard to implore her husband to come in out of the cold.

Rachel discovered her husband standing quietly near the poultry house and learned that although he had searched the area carefully he had been unable to discover anything out of the ordinary although the fowls continued to be restless.

Upshur and his wife then returned to the house where Rachel, standing in her bare feet, gently pushed her husband toward the door with the admonition that he should not remain outside another minute lest he catch his death of cold.

Rachel then paused and listened for a moment on a discarded old millstone that had been embedded in the earth at the foot of the steps. Hearing no further disturbance from the poultry house, she turned to follow her husband into the house.

At that moment a rabid fox darted from under the steps and bit Rachel viciously on one of her heels, causing her to bleed profusely on the worn surface of the old millstone.

Nine days later Rachel Upshur was seized with hydrophobia, and, as there was then no known cure for the disease, she was smothered to death with a feather bed on Christmas Day, 1749, at the instigation of her grieving husband, to put her out of her misery.

Rachel was buried in the family graveyard at Warwick and a holly tree was planted at the head of her grave. In later years, the tree grew to such a proportion it enfolded and lifted the tombstone from the ground, a process that was only stopped by the death of the tree a few years ago.

Four years after Rachel's death, Abel Upshur died, regretting to the last that he had disregarded his wife's prophetic dream sufficiently to have forbidden her to follow him when he went out to investigate the disturbance in the poultry house. Be that as it may, that is not the end of the story.

The old millstone on which Rachel Upshur bled on that long-gone winter night is still at Warwick. What is more, although it is a dull, solid gray color in dry weather, when it rains or when water is poured on it a great irregular dark red stain suddenly appears where Rachel bled when she was bitten by the rabid fox after she ignored the warning of the nightmare specter with upraised arms.

About The Author

George Holbert Tucker was born in the Berkley section of Norfolk, Virginia on September 14, 1909. He began writing features for Norfolk's *Virginian-Pilot* newspaper in 1947, and his "Tidewater Landfalls" was a popular column from its 1959 inception until Mr. Tucker's retirement from the newspaper in 1976. Two collections of his columns have been published, tales of growing up and coming-of-age in the South in the first half of the twentieth century.

A continuing student of human nature and Virginia history, Mr. Tucker has collected for *Virginia Supernatural Tales: Ghosts, Witches and Eerie Doings* some of the most fascinating stories of unusual occurrences in the Old Dominion, all of them "documented" by people who claim to have observed the mysterious circumstances or their effects.

Mr. Tucker is the author of the critically-acclaimed *A Goodly Heritage: A History of Jane Austen's Family* (1983) and contributed several articles to *The Jane Austen Companion* (1986). He presently writes a weekly column on Virginiana in the Sunday *Virginian-Pilot/Ledger-Star*.